Mac didn't know who the leggy blonde was, exactly.

Except that her name was Rita.

It didn't really matter—shouldn't really matter—but it did somehow.

Admittedly she was a pretty woman. But there was more to it than that.

She wasn't afraid to look him right in the eyes. And if she was put off by his appearance he certainly couldn't tell.

He'd never met a woman quite like her before. She was so...in control. She deliberately pushed his buttons, and she didn't care if he knew it. If anything, she dared him to do something about it.

And the problem was, Mac *wanted* to do something about it.

And he spent an inordinate amount of time fantasizing about exactly *what* that would be....

Dear Reader,

This month, Silhouette Special Edition presents an exciting selection of stories about forever love, fanciful weddings—and the warm bonds of family.

Longtime author Gina Wilkins returns to Special Edition with *Her Very Own Family,* which is part of her FAMILY FOUND: SONS & DAUGHTERS series. The Walker and D'Alessandro clans first captivated readers when they were introduced in the author's original Special Edition series, FAMILY FOUND. In this new story, THAT SPECIAL WOMAN! Brynn Larkin's life is about to change when she finds herself being wooed by a drop-dead gorgeous surgeon....

The heroines in these next three books are destined for happiness—or are they? First, Susan Mallery concludes her enchanting series duet, BRIDES OF BRADLEY HOUSE, with a story about a hometown nanny who becomes infatuated with her very own *Dream Groom.* Then the rocky road to love continues with *The Long Way Home* by RITA Award-winning author Cheryl Reavis—a poignant tale about a street-smart gal who finds acceptance where she least expects it. And you won't want to miss the passionate reunion romance in *If I Only Had a... Husband* by Andrea Edwards. This book launches the fun-filled new series, THE BRIDAL CIRCLE, about four long-term friends who discover there's no place like home—to find romance!

Rounding off the month, we have *Accidental Parents* by Jane Toombs—an emotional story about an orphan who draws his new parents together. And a no-strings-attached arrangement goes awry when a newlywed couple becomes truly smitten in *Their Marriage Contract* by Val Daniels.

I hope you enjoy all our selections this month!

Sincerely,

Karen Taylor Richman
Senior Editor

Please address questions and book requests to:
Silhouette Reader Service
U.S.: 3010 Walden Ave., P.O. Box 1325, Buffalo, NY 14269
Canadian: P.O. Box 609, Fort Erie, Ont. L2A 5X3

CHERYL REAVIS
THE LONG WAY HOME

Silhouette®

SPECIAL EDITION®

Published by Silhouette Books

America's Publisher of Contemporary Romance

For Mama and Gazie

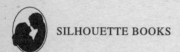 SILHOUETTE BOOKS

ISBN 0-373-24245-X

THE LONG WAY HOME

Copyright © 1999 by Cheryl Reavis

Books by Cheryl Reavis

Silhouette Special Edition

A Crime of the Heart #487
Patrick Gallagher's Widow #627
One of Our Own #901
Meggie's Baby #1039
Mother To Be #1102
Tenderly #1147
Little Darlin' #1177
The Long Way Home #1245

* Family Blessings

Harlequin Historicals
The Prisoner #126
The Bartered Bride #319
Harrigan's Bride #439

Silhouette Books

To Mother With Love 1991
"So This Is Love"

CHERYL REAVIS,

award-winning short story author and romance novelist who also writes under the name of Cinda Richards, describes herself as a "late bloomer" who played in her first piano recital at the tender age of thirty. "We had to line up by height—I was the third smallest kid," she says. "After that, there was no stopping me. I immediately gave myself permission to attempt my *other* heart's desire—to write." Her Silhouette Special Edition novel *A Crime of the Heart* reached millions of readers in *Good Housekeeping* magazine. Both *A Crime of the Heart* and *Patrick Gallagher's Widow* won the Romance Writers of America's coveted RITA Award for Best Contemporary Series Romance the year they were published. *One of Our Own* received the Career Achievement Award for Best Innovative Series Romance from *Romantic Times Magazine*. A former public health nurse, Cheryl makes her home in North Carolina with her husband.

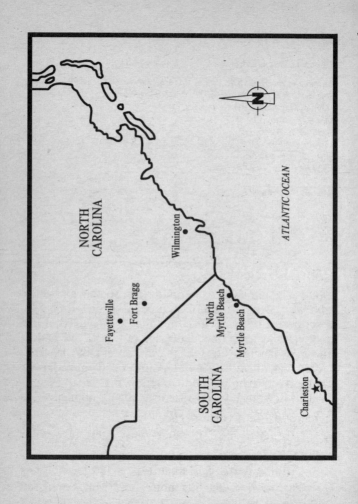

Prologue

"You can have something for the pain, Lieutenant."

The patient didn't open his eyes. In fact, he gave no indication that he was even aware that anyone else was in the room.

"Lieutenant McGraw—" a second, younger and more insistent voice began.

"He heard me," the first voice interrupted. "He doesn't want it."

"But he needs it. He can't—"

There was a rustling noise, and Mac could tell that they had both moved farther away from the bed—farther away, but not beyond his hearing.

"What he *needs* is to get this over with," the first

voice said in a lower but still authoritative tone. "And while we're at it, he needs us to stop talking about him like he's not here."

"I don't think he realizes the discomfort involved—"

"Trust me. He realizes. And it's up to him to decide whether or not he can take it. Not you and not me."

Mac still made no effort to acknowledge their presence. The fact of the matter was that he despised them both. The young one who didn't understand, and especially the old warhorse who did. She must have been in the military a long time, he thought. She must have seen a lot of things—bad things. Her relentless patience and empathy told him he was wasting his time. There was nothing he could say or do that would surprise her, because she'd seen and heard it all. Sometimes he thought she knew what his reaction would be even before he did.

And he resented her for it. He didn't want his every response anticipated as if he fit some paragraph in a medical textbook. This situation was his. The burns. The pain. The nightmares.

All *his*.

But he wasn't in a John Wayne movie and no one was going to offer him a bullet to bite. He was on his way to the showers again. The burns on his legs were going to be scrubbed raw—now—and he would have to deal with it.

He opened his eyes.

The old warhorse was holding the syringe with pain medication that would give his mind and his body ease—at least for an hour or so.

"I don't want it," he said.

"Liar," she said gently, so gently he thought he might cry.

She knows, he thought, regardless of all her talk about giving him a choice. She knew that he wanted to hurt, needed to hurt, and at the same time needed the dignity of not making a sound. Maybe she even knew why. Maybe he could ask her right now, and she could explain it to him.

His gaze briefly met hers and then slid away.

Chapter One

Nothing has changed, Rita Warren thought. She kept watching both sides of the Boulevard as she drove along, not really knowing what she expected to see. This stretch of road had looked the same—been the same—for as long as she could remember. It was like an irrepressible old lady who wouldn't behave at the family reunion. No matter who objected, she just kept singing her bawdy songs. So what if she was crass and a bit obscene. It didn't matter. It never mattered—she was still profitable enough to get away with it.

Because it was a weekday, nearly every vehicle Rita encountered seemed to be occupied by military personnel. She didn't see anyone she recognized.

There was a time when she could hardly go any-where in this town without someone calling to her from an open car window or a boulevard parking lot.

Hey! Ready Rita!

It suddenly occurred to her that it was she who was not the same. She wasn't "Ready Rita," the most notorious club dancer on the boulevard, any-more. She might still look like her, even dance like her, but that was all. She had money now, for one thing. Not a lot by some standards, but more than she'd ever thought possible. And, for the first time in her life, she was actually experiencing the self-satisfaction that came from having had a long-held dream come true. Oddly enough, it was this remark-able occurrence that had led her to finally face all the other things in her life she wasn't so satisfied about.

Money, success, a certain kind of fame from do-ing what she loved best in the world, what she had literally sacrificed her rights to her daughter to have, had precipitated a kind of epiphany. An attack of insight that let her look into the dressing-room mir-ror one day and know exactly what kind of person she was—and wasn't. The "dream come true" of performing in Las Vegas suddenly became two shows a day, six days a week, twenty-five pounds of feathers and fifteen pounds of jewelry—and no baby daughter. The remarkable achievement of hav-ing gone to an open audition and actually having been hired to dance in one of the most famous and prestigious shows in Vegas didn't help. The accolades from the audience didn't help. The six hundred dollars a week—and then more—didn't help. She had thought she could just walk away and forget the mess she'd made of her life, but that hadn't been the case. She'd soon realized that whatever she decided to do with her newfound, elevated consciousness, she had to have capital. She rounded up several of the other dancers—college students, single mothers and the like—who needed to save every penny and talked some of them into sharing an apartment.

She already knew how to live on practically nothing, and now, driven by the need to backtrack and make things right once and for all, she absolutely excelled at saving money. *Now*—she was more or less sitting pretty. Or at least pretty enough to be able to come home again. She knew there were people who would think she had crawled back here with her tail between her legs, that she had had her shot at the Big Time, and failed. She knew there were people who would think it ludicrous that she— Ready Rita—had not only returned but was going to go to school at the local community college. She didn't care. She couldn't fix the situation until she had fixed herself. If she wanted to be an important part of her daughter's life, then she had to be worthy of it.

Olivia was happy with her father and his new wife. As much as Rita would have liked to believe otherwise, she knew that to be true. She couldn't just show up on Matt and Corey Beltran's doorstep and announce that she'd had second thoughts and now felt like being Olivia's mother again. She loved her baby girl—regardless of the way it may have appeared. She had no excuses for her past behavior—except that it now seemed as if it had all happened to someone else.

She had done an incredibly stupid thing in leaving Olivia with her soldier father the way she had, and she was paying for that mistake. But that didn't mean that she had to leave everything exactly as it was. She could still see Olivia. Matt and Corey wouldn't deny her that. And if she took it slowly, carefully, there was a good chance she could participate in her baby's life again. To participate, not to disrupt. That was all she wanted. Just to be there for Olivia and have her know that her mother loved her.

A pickup truck abruptly changed lanes in front of her, and Rita reached out to keep her stack of textbooks from sliding onto the floor. Even she found it hard to believe that she was actually going back to school. But she was fully convinced that the community college wouldn't be like high school. She would no longer be intimidated by not belonging to the in crowd, by not feeling pretty enough, or rich enough or smart enough to even try. She was going to soar now—she hoped—in spite of her impetuous decision to take a course in algebra instead of business math.

At the moment, though, she had other things on her mind. She wanted to see her baby girl. Finally. She'd taken care of business first—taken care of finding a place to live and enrolling in school. She was still looking for some kind of gainful employment, but she knew exactly what she wanted to do about that. And now she was ready to take on the scary prospect of presenting herself to her daughter. She had called Matt's house several times today, but no one had answered the phone. On impulse she decided to go by anyway.

She turned off the boulevard onto the street that ran past the yellow house on the corner where her daughter lived. There were no cars in the driveway, but she still stopped, her heart aching at the sight of the little red-and-blue tricycle on the front porch. She had sent it to Olivia for her birthday, the big "zero-three." Corey Beltran had told her that Olivia liked it. Maybe it was true. It certainly looked... appreciated.

Rita smiled abruptly to herself, imagining the little girl Olivia must be now, zipping around on her first set of "wheels." She wondered if Olivia would even know her. Corey had sent her pictures faithfully, all kinds of pictures. Olivia in her Sunday best. Dirty-faced Olivia after a hard day in the sandbox. Olivia sleeping on Matt's shoulder at the military's Fourth of July celebration. And Rita had returned the favor with a publicity photo that featured her in all her showgirl glory—bosom covered, in case the

Beltrans, or anyone else who happened to see it, still thought of her as ''that'' kind of dancer.

Her smile abruptly faded. She had missed so much of Olivia's life.

''And whose fault is that, Rita?'' she whispered, knowing exactly where to lay the blame. She sat there, staring at the yellow house, the front porch with the swing and the ivy and the hanging baskets of red geraniums.

The place looked exactly like what it was—home, something Rita had experienced only briefly before her grandmother had died. She could remember riding past houses like this one when she was a little girl, wishing—wishing so *hard*—that she could live in one, not because of the house itself but because of the love and caring that surely must be inside. She had firmly believed that houses like these—the ones with tricycles and flowers on the porch—were places where little girls were looked after. There would be sit-down meals with a mother *and* a father, and clean clothes, and people who cared if they were hungry or sick or scared. And—

And if she wasn't careful, she was going to be bawling about her poor, pitiful childhood in a minute, when she'd learned a long time ago there was no point in it. What mattered now was Olivia's childhood, not hers. She couldn't change the past, and in lieu of sitting there feeling sorry for herself, she abruptly decided to leave a note. She got out of the car, and she had walked nearly to the front door when another car pulled in behind hers.

Matt.

She saw immediately the change in his expression as he realized who she was. It was clear that he still expected the absolute worst from her—and not without good reason. But he was the kind of man who met his problems head-on. He approached her with the same kind of grim determination he must use whenever he found himself in the Balkans or Haiti or any of the other places he'd been sent to keep the peace. The same determination he'd had after he'd learned that he was Olivia's father—whether he remembered the occasion or not. Watching him now, it surprised Rita to note that her unrequited passion for him had somehow dissipated during the time she'd been away. The passion, but not the respect.

"Rita," he said by way of greeting, and nothing more, his expression still wary. She remembered suddenly the way his face would light up whenever he saw his wife. Someday, she wanted a man to look at *her* the way she'd seen Matt look at Corey. She wondered if he still did that, still looked at the woman he'd married with the unabashed eyes of love. Probably—or he wouldn't be so obviously worried now.

"Sergeant," she said just as gravely, then smiled. He didn't smile in return.

Okay, then, she thought. *If that's how it's going to be.*

"I came to see Olivia," she said.

"She's not here."

"When will she be back?"

"I don't know."

"You don't *know?*"

"That's what I said."

"Why not, Matt?" Rita asked pointedly, because she was becoming more than a little annoyed by his reluctance to tell her anything. She wasn't just somebody in off the street here. She was Olivia's real mother, and he'd do well to remember that. "I came to see my baby. It's in the custody agreement. You do know that much?"

"Well, you missed her. Sorry."

"Yeah, I can see how sorry you are. But if you don't want me—and my lawyer—on your doorstep every day, you'd better tell me where she is and when she's coming home."

"Are you going to be in town awhile?" he asked, completely unimpressed by the ultimatum.

"A *long* while," she said, and if she thought he had looked less than delighted to see her before, it was nothing compared to now.

Welcome home, Rita.

"Are you going to give me a little hint about when she'll be here, or not?"

"I told you. I don't know—not for sure. When I talk to Corey, I'll ask her."

"You do that. You and Corey aren't having problems, are you? Is that why you're so…uninformed?

If Olivia is in the middle of some kind of marital trouble here—''

"There isn't any marital trouble, Rita. Corey and the kids went with her parents to the beach. Her father had a heart attack a few weeks ago. He was afraid he wouldn't ever see the ocean again, and he insisted he was going. Corey went along to do the driving. How long they stay will depend on him—on how well he gets along while he's there. She calls every night. I'll tell her you came by."

"And I want to know when Olivia's coming back.''

"That, too. Anything else?"

"No, that's all—except, I don't know why you're acting like this."

"Experience, Rita. Experience."

She sighed. She had no legitimate argument for that. "So is...Olivia okay?" she asked after a moment.

"She's fine," he said shortly.

She looked up at him. He was still worried.

"She's...fine," he repeated, a little less defensively this time.

"What about the other one?" she asked, and he looked at her blankly. She knew perfectly well why. He hadn't expected her to be civil. A conversation with Rita Warren surely wouldn't include chitchat and pleasantries.

"The other kid, Matt," she said in spite of her insight and with more sarcasm than she really intended. "The one you and Corey had, remember? Olivia's half brother. How is he?"

"He's fine."

"Now that you've got the little prince, does that mean you're not going to care all that much about Olivia? Because if it does—"

"Rita! I love both my children. *Both* of them, okay!"

"Okay," she said lightly. "Don't get so pushed out of shape. I have to ask, don't I?"

He didn't answer her. He just stood there, obviously wishing her gone.

"I'm going," she assured him. "But I'll call tomorrow. And if I don't get an answer, I'll be back."

"Hey," he said when she was about to open the car door. "Have you been to see Bugs Doyle?"

"No, why?" she asked, surprised by the question. She and Spec 4 Calvin "Bugs" Doyle had come to a parting of the ways even before she left for the greener pastures of Las Vegas. Surely Matt knew that.

"I know you two were close—"

"We were *not* 'close.' Not the way *you* mean. He helped me out when nobody else would. That's *all*. And if you—"

"All right!" he said, holding up both hands. "I was just going to tell you he's still in the hospital—"

"Still? What do you mean 'still'?"

"He was on a Black Hawk that went down on a

night training mission. Maybe you ought to go see him. I don't think he gets many visitors.''

Rita looked at him. ''Is he hurt...bad?''

''Bad enough. He and his lieutenant were the only ones who made it.''

''I hate hospitals,'' she said.

''Suit yourself.''

''What is that supposed to mean?'' she asked, immediately offended by the tone of his voice.

''Nothing, Rita—but you're the one who said the man helped you out.''

''Did I say I wouldn't go see him? I didn't say I wouldn't *go*. I just said I hate hospitals. I have ever since that time when Olivia was so sick. You are so hard to get along with—I don't know how Corey stands you.''

For the first time, he almost smiled.

''Don't you forget to ask Corey about Olivia,'' she said, opening the car door.

''You're going to go see Bugs?''

''Yes! I'm going to go see him!''

''Good. If anybody can take his mind off his troubles, you can.''

She gave him a look before she got into the car. His heavy-handed implication was that she was such a handful Bugs would be forced to forget his current miseries because he'd have to deal with her.

To her surprise, Matt actually smiled this time, and for one brief moment she felt that old longing for what might have been.

I hope you know how lucky you are, Corey, she thought as she drove away.

It was late afternoon before she made it to the hospital. It wasn't the same hospital where Olivia had been admitted when she'd had scarlet fever. This was the new one with an odd kind of architectural style that reminded Rita of an airport terminal-slash-Oriental pagoda. But she still remembered that terrible time whether she wanted to or not. She had felt so lost and helpless then. Everything in her life had spiraled completely out of control. Olivia had been so desperately sick, and Rita had had absolutely no say in anything. She was not the ''custodial parent,'' and the doctors completely ignored her. *Everyone* ignored her—except Corey Beltran.

Rita had no one to blame but herself, of course, but even she could appreciate the absurdity of finding herself keeping a bedside vigil for Olivia with Matt's new wife. *He* was off peacekeeping. They had cried together, prayed together. For Olivia's sake, she and Corey Beltran had stood strong. Nearly losing that little girl had been a horrible experience for them all—from which Rita had learned two very important truths. Matt Beltran loved his daughter. And Matt Beltran did *not* love Rita Warren.

She gave a quiet sigh. The torch she had once carried for him was definitely out.

Well, okay, she thought. *Maybe it's still smoking—just a little.*

And it was for that reason as much as any that she was going make this visit. Sergeant Mateo Beltran was the kind of man who took an interest in other people's welfare. Even hers. Bugs Doyle was a good man, though seeing him again might be awkward. But if Matt thought Bugs ought to have visitors, then she would oblige.

She took a deep breath and walked briskly toward the hospital main entrance, enjoying a soft summer breeze on her face and garnering an appreciative glance or two from the soldiers she encountered along the way. It had taken her a long, *long* time to realize that she might be fine just the way she was and that she didn't *have* to be dancing in a boulevard club or on a Las Vegas stage to get a man's attention. Yet another big revelation in her quest to become whole.

As she got off the elevator on the floor where Bugs was supposed to be, she was immediately struck by the fact that hospitals—new or old—all smelled alike, awash in unidentifiable food smells.

She had no trouble locating Bugs Doyle. He was sitting in a big room, alone, looking out the window, his back toward the door. She could see that both his hands and forearms were heavily bandaged and in some kind of splints that kept his hands partially open. One leg was in a cast and extended straight out in front of him. He didn't hear her when she came in, and she stood waiting until he finally looked around.

"Whoa!" he said, taken completely by surprise. "Rita! What are you doing here!"

"I came to see you, silly," she said, smiling and trying not to stare at the damage done to his face, as well. He looked as if he had a very bad sunburn—except for the fact that his eyebrows were gone. He still had his eager, boyish grin. She had no doubt that he was happy to see her, but she wondered about Matt's assertion that he hadn't had many visitors. The Bugs Doyle she knew was by no means a loner. It suddenly occurred to her that all his buddies might have been on the Black Hawk with him.

"When did you get back?" he asked. "God, you look—outstanding!"

"Yeah?" she said, doing a little pirouette so there would be no mistaking exactly how outstanding she looked. "Are you—"

Her question was interrupted by a sudden commotion from the room across the hall—raised voices. No, one raised voice and then the bouncing thud of something falling—or being thrown.

"What in the world?" she said, walking to the door.

"That's the lieutenant—Rita, don't go out there. He's having a bad day—"

Rita kept going. One of the hospital staff—a scared young girl who didn't look old enough to have the job—came rushing out of the room and into the hallway, just ahead of a flying wastepaper basket. The girl stood there for a moment, trying not to cry in the wake of the loud profanity that accompanied her abrupt exit. Lieutenant Whoever-he-was had quite a repertoire. Rita would have thought she were back on the boulevard on a raucous Saturday night three hours after the troops got paid. She could hear Bugs behind her.

"Rita? Don't—okay? Rita!"

But she didn't stop. She didn't even hesitate. She couldn't abide a bully no matter what his excuse happened to be, and she'd been caught in her share of bar fights. She wasn't about to be deterred by flying words or flying trash cans.

She stepped into the room, flinging the door much wider than was necessary.

"Get out!" the patient yelled at her, looking hard for something else to throw. He, like Bugs, was sitting in a wheelchair—only he was *not* happy about it. Both his legs were extended in front of him and there were bandages instead of a cast. The only thing he could reach was a magazine. He flung it hard, and the effort clearly caused him pain. Rita caught it in midair and flung it right back at him. It hit his left shoulder and slid to his lap.

"Come on. Give it your best shot," she said, because clearly he was thinking about letting the magazine fly again. "What?" she asked when he didn't immediately take her up on her offer. "You only want to dish it out to somebody who *has* to take it?

Who do you think you are? Oh, yeah, I remember. You're the guy having the *bad* day—''

''I want out of the goddamned chair!'' he yelled. ''If you're not going to help me, then get out! You don't know—''

''What?'' she interrupted. ''You've been hurt? Well, big deal! If you really want to make some kind of a statement, I'll go see if I can find somebody with a little rank for you to take it out on—that way you won't have to pick on a terrified kid. You may not believe this, but there are still a few of us on the planet who have problems of our own and we really don't care what kind of day *you're* having. So stop whining and get on with it!''

She turned and made her exit, expecting to be hit by the magazine all the way out the door. She found Bugs trying desperately to move his wheelchair with his bandaged hands.

''Man, Rita!'' he said when he saw her. ''What did you go and do that for!''

''What?'' she asked innocently.

''He's an officer, for God's sake! You shouldn't have done that.''

''No, *he* shouldn't have done that. I'm not one of his underlings.''

''You can't just go telling him off like that!''

''Bugs, I've already done it. Take it easy, will you?''

He stared at her for a moment, then gave a sharp sigh. ''Damn, Rita, you are something else.''

"Well, don't bother telling me what."

He suddenly grinned. "No, I mean it. I'm... impressed."

"Why? Because I said what needed saying?"

"No," he said, teasing now. "Because you didn't swear. Who *are* you and what have you done with the real Rita Warren?"

"Very funny," she said, but the truth was she hadn't even thought about swearing. *Not* swearing was all part of the new and improved version of herself, a little something extra she'd learned in Las Vegas right along with the dance routines. The show's program manager had absolutely forbidden profanity in her presence. She intended that her dancers be a cut above the rest in more ways than just their choreography.

"My dancers are the best!" she'd say. "And you're going to act like it!"

Those guilty of offending her were fined—five dollars a word. And for once Rita hadn't wanted to go head-to-head with the person in authority. The job was too important. Succeeding was too important. Not to mention the fact that she couldn't spare the five bucks.

"So what about him?" she said abruptly, jerking her head in the direction of the room across the hall. "Why is he acting like that? He's not hurt as bad as you are, is he?"

Bugs shrugged, his expression suddenly closed. "He's been through a rough time."

"And you haven't?"

"He's got the responsibility."

"For what?"

Bugs made no attempt to answer her.

"For what?" she insisted.

"For...the ones who didn't make it."

"He was flying the Black Hawk?"

"No, he wasn't flying the Black Hawk."

"Then how is he responsible?"

"Rita, you're a civilian. You don't understand."

"So explain it to me."

He looked at her, but he made no attempt to elaborate.

"It's not just that," he said after a moment. "I think he's having trouble with his fiancée."

"What kind of trouble?"

"Army life just ain't her cup of tea. Every time she comes here—even before he was hurt—she always acts like she thinks she's been dropped in the middle of an insane asylum."

Rita gave him a pointed look, and he grinned.

"It ain't *that* bad," he assured her.

"You think?" she said, still teasing.

"Yeah, I think. Anyway, there's her—and then his mama's been raising hell."

"About the fiancée?" Rita asked, blatantly looking for an interesting angle. She had seen some of these women who were "career army" because their husbands were and who thought *his* rank extended to her. Of course, for all intents and purposes, it did.

She could see how a woman like that might not approve of a potential daughter-in-law who was less than enamored with the prospect of becoming an army wife.

"No, about the kind of care the lieutenant is getting. It ain't up to her standards. See, she's not too happy about his career choice, either. I think she'd rather have a daughter in a whorehouse than him in the army. It's bad enough he's in the military—and then to have him end up like he is. It just ain't in keeping with the money."

"What money?"

"His mama's rich. And she's used to getting her way. *She* wanted him to stay in the hospital in San Antonio and when they sent him back here, she got some senator or somebody to rattle a few cages. And then the lieutenant…he wouldn't do what she wanted—so now she comes here and raises hell just like clockwork—making sure her boy gets what she needs."

"What *she* needs?"

"Yeah. It's her wanting all this extra stuff done— not him. Lieutenant McGraw—he's okay, you know?"

"If you say so."

"Well, you can't go by today. I don't think the fiancée is going to show up. She's been here every day since he got here. Today—no fiancée. He ain't taking it too well, see? It ain't easy having the one you want go off someplace else."

He looked at her, then away. She didn't say anything and neither did he, both of them choosing not to drag all that out again. He had once wanted a lot more from her than she had been able to give, and for once in her life, she had taken charge of a situation and told him the truth up-front. He'd been good to her when she needed help, and she would always be grateful—but she didn't feel *that* way about him and she wouldn't pretend otherwise. In the long run, she thought he appreciated it.

She didn't press him for more information. She was thinking about McGraw himself. For the briefest of moments he had allowed her to look into his eyes, and she'd seen all that anger and all that misery. It was a lethal and self-destructive combination. Nobody knew that better than she did. And somebody ought to tell him so.

Chapter Two

"Hey! Are you going to leave me in here? How long does it take to get a damned wheelchair! Hey!"

McGraw waited impatiently for someone to answer him, clinging to the cold tile wall, the pain from the latest shower and scrubbing excruciating. He felt light-headed, nauseous.

Abandoned.

"Hey!" he yelled again. He could not *believe* this. His whole life had come down to wheelchairs and begging to either get out or in.

A nurse—*the* nurse—finally pushed open the door.

"What is it, Lieutenant?" she asked calmly.

"Where is the damned wheelchair!"

"No wheelchair," she said.

"What do you mean, no wheelchair? Where is it! I'm ready to go back!"

"Then go," she said, turning to leave.

"Wait!" he cried. "What do you think you're doing!"

"I'm leaving you here, Lieutenant. You aren't doing anything to help yourself so we've decided to do it for you. Since you're determined to let your burns heal in all the wrong places, you are hereby declared ambulatory. You get back the best way you can."

"Wait! Wait— You can't do that!"

She didn't wait. She didn't even hesitate. She just…left him.

He went after her, his rage driving him forward, lurching, trying to walk, pulling loose the half-healed places they were so concerned about with every step. He made it to the door, then into the hallway. She stood waiting for him at the far end, her hands resting serenely on her hips. He had to hold on to the wall to keep from falling, but he kept going, venting his anger with every appropriate word he could think of.

"What! You think this is funny!" he yelled at her in the middle of his tirade.

No, of course she didn't think it was funny. She didn't think anything, damn her!

He kept going—until he was so out of breath that he had to stop. He stood there, leaning against the wall, nearly bent double in the effort it took not to feel the pain in his legs and to breathe.

"I want the damned wheelchair!" he yelled at her and anyone else who might be within hearing. "Did you hear me!"

I can't stand this!

It hurt so *bad.* He clenched his teeth, but the tears still ran down his face.

Someone was coming, but he made no effort to look up.

Finally!

But the feet that came into view weren't hospital feet. They weren't even military. These feet were wearing sexy little high-heeled sandals. Red snakeskin, for God's sake. Nothing but a strap or two over the beautifully manicured toes and one around the ankle. He could see how soft and smooth the legs were. The light scent of...almonds and...cherries wafted around him. He immediately looked up and directly into *her* eyes. Doyle's tall blonde, back again, and no more impressed than she'd been at their first meeting.

"I'm just never going to see you at your best, am I?" she said, but she gave him no time to answer, not even profanely. She walked away, completely oblivious to his suffering. Heretofore, he had thought that unsolicited sympathy and understanding annoyed him. He was wrong. *This* annoyed him. Doyle's blonde didn't feel sorry for him. There was no mistaking that. She was giving him exactly the indifference he thought he wanted.

In spite of all he could do, he watched her go. He watched the way her hips swayed and her short skirt—a filmy white, dangerous skirt with little red rosebuds on it—swirled around her long legs.

He watched as she turned the corner and disappeared, but he could still mark her progress down the corridor, because he could hear the appreciative whistles and shouts that came as she passed each open doorway. Good-looking women came into this place all the time, but none of them precipitated that kind of response.

Who the hell is *she?*

But he had no time to ponder that riddle. He couldn't hold the pain at bay any longer. It swept over him suddenly, taking every ounce of strength he had. His legs were shaking. It was all he could do to stay on his feet and to keep from bawling like a little kid.

The warhorse was there suddenly, taking him by the arm and helping him into the wheelchair he couldn't beg, borrow or steal earlier.

"You did good, Lieutenant," she said. "You're bleeding through your bandages some, but I expect you've just saved yourself a fair amount of surgery."

He was too exhausted to tell her what she could do with her assessment of the situation.

"Come on," she said. "Let's get you put back

where you belong. You wouldn't want Miss Bradner to see you like this.''

He glanced at her. Whatever else the warhorse might know, he didn't think she knew about his personal life.

Joanna.

He had to do something about Joanna. He had known her since they were both children, and he could see through all her forced cheerfulness. The way she never quite looked at him, never wanted to meet his eyes. She was too well-bred to throw a magazine at him when he showed his frustration, but he was still convinced that if he suggested that they call everything off, she would take him up on it. She was a good person, a caring person, but she hadn't wanted to be—as his mother so indelicately put it—''a camp follower.'' It was hard enough for her when he had insisted on a career in the military instead of going to law school and joining his grandfather's law firm. It was even worse that he had ended up in this condition because of it.

Nothing was turning out the way she had planned. He thought that she must be finding her current moral dilemma very difficult. She *wanted* to stay with him no matter what, but she hadn't bargained for *this*. If he gave her the opportunity, she would simply accept their situation as he presented it— hopeless—and politely withdraw. She would return the ruby and diamond engagement ring that had be-

longed to his grandmother and that would be it. End
of engagement. End of story.

"Okay, Lieutenant," the warhorse said.

He looked around at her. She'd gotten her hands
on yet another syringe with pain medication.

"I don't want—"

"Shut up!" she said, and in spite of his agony he
smiled. He'd finally done it. He'd finally made the
old warhorse lose her cool.

"What happened—to all that—big talk about letting me—decide?" he asked as she none too gently
found a place midthigh and jabbed the needle home.
He didn't resist. His capitulation was total, but he
still had to have the last word.

"That was then. Now you're worn-out and you're
going to sleep—"

"I never sleep."

"You will this time. And that's that!"

"Yes, mother," he said dutifully.

"You better be glad I'm not your mother," she
said. "I'd crack that hard head of yours."

"What's wrong?" Bugs asked immediately.

"Nothing," Rita said, forgetting for a moment
that this was Bugs, who knew her only too well.
The truth was that she'd been down all day and finding McGraw in the hall in that condition hadn't
helped. She hadn't been able to get Matt on the
phone, and she was very much afraid that it wasn't
a coincidence. She wanted to see Olivia; she'd come

all this way to see her. All the wonderful self-assurance that had made her see things so clearly before seemed to have dissipated now. And so far she had absolutely nothing to show for her efforts and good intentions.

She managed a smile. "So how's it going?"

"It's going. That's about it. Did you get tangled up in whatever that was with the lieutenant?"

"Not really. One of the nurses told me what was going on when I got off the elevator—in case I wanted to come back later. But I didn't see any reason not to walk by him. It's not like I don't know what he's like when he's…upset."

"So what was going on?"

Rita gave a small sigh, still trying to get McGraw's tortured face out of her mind. "The nurse said he wouldn't move around like he was supposed to and the places on the backs of his knees were healing wrong. So they had to *make* him move around. They stranded him without a wheelchair. The nurse said he had too much pride not to try to make it on his own, but it wasn't a pretty sight."

"You didn't say anything to him," he said, clearly worried.

She didn't answer him.

"Rita, you didn't, did you?"

"I didn't say anything much, okay?"

"Rita! I keep telling you—"

"Yes, I know. He's an officer. He's had a bad

time. And maybe his fiancée is planning to dump him—"

"You didn't say anything about *that,* did you?"

"No," she said defensively.

He didn't say anything else, and she glanced at him. He was sitting there, staring at nothing. It occurred to her that maybe she *had* taken his mind off his immediate troubles.

"You okay?" she asked.

"Yeah. Yeah, I'm okay." He abruptly smiled. "So, how's the baby girl?"

"I don't know. I haven't seen her. She's at the beach indefinitely with Corey."

"How long has it been—since you saw her last?"

"Ten months," she said. *Eight days. Sixteen hours.*

"She a good-looking little kid," he said, shifting his weight in his wheelchair.

"Is she?" There was a slight quiver in her voice in spite of all she could do.

"Hey—" he said, reaching toward her with a bandaged hand. "If you need money—"

"No, I don't need money. I just miss Olivia, that's all."

"When are you going back to Vegas?"

"I'm not. I'm staying here."

He looked at her. "You got a job?"

"No, not yet. I'm looking into some things."

"Well, I can let you have a little cash if—"

"I don't need your money, Bugs," she said, smiling. "Really."

"You going back to dancing at the club?"

"Nope. I'm going to school."

"Yeah? For what?"

"To pick up where I left off. I'm going to get the General Equivalency Diploma and then we'll see. And I'm going to start my own business—exercise classes—something with a little Las Vegas flavor."

He laughed.

"I'm serious," she insisted. "I learned a lot of routines—I might as well use them. People get tired of the same old, same old. I'm going to hit women right where their showgirl fantasies live. I've just got to find a place to set up shop—"

She abruptly stopped. He didn't say anything.

"I really can do this."

"Hey, I believe you. You always could make it happen."

She didn't say anything, because it wasn't true, and they both knew it. She certainly hadn't been able to "make it happen" where she and Matt Beltran were concerned. Nothing had gone right, and no one knew that any better than Bugs did. He'd been there through the worst of it, patiently helping her pick up the pieces.

"Does Beltran know you're back?" he asked after a moment.

"Yes and no," she said, but she didn't want to

get into that. "Hey, Airborne. Let's go for a walk. I'll push. You ride."

"Outstanding," he said. "You wouldn't happen to have a cold beer on you, would you?"

"Not this trip," she said significantly, and he laughed.

"You're all right, you know that?"

"Darned straight," she said to make him laugh again. And she'd be the first to admit that her "all right-ness" had been a long time coming. She wouldn't think about how fragile it had been today. She bent to release the brakes on the wheelchair.

"And you look good, girl. Did I say that?"

"A couple of days ago."

"Yeah, well, you still do. Damned good."

She smiled. "Where to, big guy?"

"Let's make the rounds," he said.

But he didn't mean "make the rounds." He meant "check on his lieutenant." And he meant for her to go to see if McGraw was receiving visitors.

"Bugs, are you sure?" she asked for the second time. Bugs hadn't seen the man stranded in the hall earlier.

"Yeah, I'm sure. This is the New Army. Officers are supposed to be accessible. See if I can talk to him, okay? I got a message for him."

"What kind of message?"

"One of the guys who…didn't make it—I talked to his grandmother on the phone a couple of weeks ago. She wanted me to tell the lieutenant something.

You go and see if I can talk to him—but don't get him all stirred up.''

"I'm not going to get him stirred up. I don't—"

"I mean it, Rita. This is important."

"Then why don't you go? The 'New Army' and all that."

"Because this is…different. It ain't nothing official. I just want to tell him what she said."

"Why haven't you told him before?"

"Because there hasn't been any 'before.'"

"You mean, he's right across the hall and you haven't talked to him since—"

"Just go see, okay?"

"Okay," she said, but she mentally prepared herself to have to bob and weave.

"And don't stir him up."

"Okay! I got that part."

McGraw's door was standing slightly ajar, and she hesitated for a moment before she looked in. She didn't knock, because after that ordeal in the hall, she thought he might be sleeping. He was in bed, lying on his stomach, his face turned away. She started to leave, but then he turned his head toward her.

They stared at each other. Or she stared at him. He was looking at her legs.

"What do you want?" he asked finally.

"Magazines," she said. "Trash cans."

He frowned. "What?"

"Bugs wants to come in and see you for a minute. I thought I'd disarm you first."

He didn't say anything. Clearly, he was in no mood for her brand of humor.

"Spec 4 Calvin Doyle." She plunged on. "You remember him. He didn't die, either."

The look on his face told her it was a good thing there was nothing within easy reach or she'd be playing "Think Fast" again. It also told her that with that one remark, she'd uncovered the place that really hurt, the one he was trying to keep anyone from finding out about and the one he didn't want to be treated for. She had no credentials whatsoever, but she'd seen enough soldiers like him to recognize the problem.

Good old survivor's guilt.

It was the reason she had a baby daughter, and it was the reason Matt Beltran didn't even remember the night they had made her.

"So?" she asked pointedly. "Is the lieutenant receiving or shall I extend his sincere regrets?"

"What you can do, lady, is—"

"Oh, I'm sorry!" someone said. "Am I interrupting?"

Rita looked around. A dark-haired young woman stood just behind her. She was well-dressed and pretty, and she was smiling—but in no way did she mean it. She looked as though in one sweeping glance she had considered any number of reasons

Rita might be in here with Lieutenant McGraw, and she wasn't comfortable with any of them.

"Go on," Rita said to McGraw instead of responding to her question. "What is it I can do? Tell me."

"You can—" He bit down on whatever else he was going to say. The young woman stood there, looking from one of them to the other, clearly hoping this wasn't going to turn into something unpleasant. If McGraw's previous behavior was any indication, she had probably already had all the unpleasantness she could handle.

Okay, Bugs, Rita thought. *I am going to stir him up. Maybe her, too.*

"Yes?" Rita said helpfully, her attention still on McGraw. He was working hard not to say what he really wanted to say.

"You can—tell Bugs—okay. Anytime," he said finally.

"Good. I'll do that. But not now, right?" she asked, glancing at his newest arrival.

"Now is fine," he said.

"You're sure?"

"Yes. I'm sure."

"Well, then," she said brightly. She flashed them both a smile. "I'll tell him."

"Who was that?" the young woman asked when Rita was barely out the door.

"I don't know," McGraw said. "And I don't care."

It was obvious Bugs had been waiting anxiously for her to return. Whatever he had to tell McGraw *must* be important, she thought.

''What did he say?'' he asked immediately.

''He said 'anytime.'''

''Yeah? Good. Let's go then—push me, will you?''

She stood there, still thinking about McGraw's remark to his visitor, about whether or not it had actually hurt her feelings.

Yes, she thought in surprise.

''Oh, God, you stirred him up, didn't you?'' Bugs said.

''No, I didn't. If I had, he wouldn't have said 'anytime,' now would he?''

''Then let's go. I've got to get this over with.''

Rita pushed him into the hall, but not fast enough to suit him. The dark-haired woman was still in Mc-Graw's room.

''I guess we better forget this,'' Bugs said when he saw her.

''No,'' Rita said. ''She was here before. I asked him if he'd rather see you later. He said no.''

Bugs looked at her doubtfully, but she'd had enough of this. She pushed him on into the room whether he was technically off the fence about it or not. And she left immediately, then turned back as soon as she was in the hall. She moved to where neither man could see her, and crooked her finger at the young woman—who clearly thought Rita was out of her mind. Rita gave her a pointed look and crooked her finger again. This time she came—but Rita could tell she didn't want to.

Reaching behind her, Rita pulled the door almost closed, not giving her time to ask whatever question she already had her mouth pursed to ask.

"They haven't talked since the Black Hawk went down," Rita said, getting to the bottom line.

The woman looked at her. "Oh," she said finally, glancing over her shoulder at the door. "I see."

They stood there, neither of them knowing quite what to do with themselves.

"I'm…Joanna Bradner," the woman said after a moment, offering her hand.

Rita shook it. "Rita Warren."

"Is he your husband?"

"Hus—no. No, Bugs is just a friend."

They immediately ran out of topics for conversation. The awkwardness between them lengthened.

"Have you…known him long?" Joanna Bradner asked abruptly.

"Oh, I've known Bugs about—"

"No, I meant Mac."

"I don't know…*Mac* at all," Rita said, surprised by the question because she'd heard him plainly tell her that he didn't know who Rita was and didn't care.

"Oh," Joanna said again.

"Let's not dance around this," Rita said. "Go ahead and say whatever it is you want to say."

But Joanna Bradner didn't say anything, at least not for a while. Rita could hear Bugs and McGraw—Mac—talking quietly. No flying trash cans or flying words as yet.

"He's different," Joanna suddenly said, in spite of her obvious discomfort with the direction this conversation had taken.

"Well, he would be, wouldn't he? Didn't somebody talk to you about the consequences of the crash—post-traumatic stress and all that?" Rita asked.

"Yes," Joanna said.

"Well?"

"He was different before that."

Rita looked at her, trying to decide what this woman was really concerned about—or rather, what she thought Rita had to do with anything.

"Why don't you just ask him about it?" Rita suggested.

"I'm asking you."

"Well, I can't help you. I told you I don't know Lieutenant McGraw. Actually—"

She stopped, because of the woman who had come to stand a short distance away. Lou Kurian. The social worker who knew everything about Rita Warren there was to know, the good, the bad *and* the ugly.

"Lou," Rita said, stepping away from Joanna Bradner and making sure she was out of her hearing before she gave Lou the opportunity to start in.

"What are you up to now?" Lou said without prelude.

"What makes you think I'm up to something?"

"I don't think you're up to something, *she* does. Why?"

"I have no idea why."

"Uh-huh."

"I don't!" Rita insisted. "But I might have found out if you hadn't interrupted. Besides which, you shouldn't be eavesdropping in the first place."

"I can't help it if I have excellent hearing. What are you doing here, anyway?"

"I'm here to see Bugs Doyle. He was hurt—"

"Yeah, I know about Bugs. And I know about Lieutenant McGraw. I know about you, too. I repeat. What are you doing here?"

"I'm thinking of doing some volunteer work," she answered, saying the first thing that popped into her head. But she realized, even as she said it, that the idea hadn't come entirely from out of the blue. She needed something to do, and she certainly knew how to cheer men up.

Lou clutched her chest and took a step backward. "Hold on heart! She's just kidding."

"I'm not kidding," Rita said. "I'm thinking of volunteering."

"Between shows?" Lou asked pointedly.

"I'm not doing that now," Rita said evenly. She absolutely refused to be annoyed by Lou's so-called humor.

"Here or in Vegas?"

"Both—and why are you giving me such a hard time!"

"Because you always gave *me* a hard time. You never kept your appointments, you never told me the truth—"

"I did so tell you the truth—it was the truth when I said it, anyway. I couldn't help it if what I thought would happen didn't."

Lou stared at her. "Uh-huh," she said again. "You know what? This would be a whole lot easier if I didn't like you. So, are you back to stay or what?"

"I'm back to stay."

"Back and all ready to upset Olivia's life, I take it. Not to mention *mine*."

"No, I'm not going to upset Olivia's life. I want to see her, yes. I have the right to see her. It's not going to be like before. I'm going to get a job, and I've already enrolled in school—"

"School," Lou said.

"Yes, school! You're the one who used to keep after me about it!"

"So I did. School. Well, that's good, Rita. You stick with it and—"

Rita held up her hands. "No lecture. Please."

Lou smiled. "I'll try to hold back, but, child, it's what I *do*. Just try to keep your personal life straight, okay?"

"What personal life would that be, Lou?"

Lou glanced at Joanna Bradner who still stood outside McGraw's door.

"Lou, I told you—"

"Okay! And I am out of line—just a little. You take care of yourself. I'll see you around. I expect our paths will cross."

Rita watched her walk away. She expected that their paths would cross, too—but she wasn't here to cause trouble, no matter what Lou Kurian thought.

Joanna Bradner was no longer standing in the hall. Rita waited a moment before she pushed open the door to McGraw's room. The men were still talking. She could hear Bugs plainly.

"Sir, yes, Sir," he said. "Rita was just being Rita."

Chapter Three

McGraw still looked up whenever anyone passed the door, but after more than a week of keeping a vigil he never would have admitted keeping, he had more or less decided that Doyle's blonde wouldn't be coming back. He hadn't seen her since she'd whisked the soldier out of the room with a good deal more haste than was necessary. He hadn't seen Doyle, either, but even if he had, McGraw wouldn't have asked him about her conspicuous absence.

Or maybe it wasn't conspicuous. Maybe a visit or two was all she had ever intended. He still didn't know who she was exactly. Or more precisely, who she *thought* she was. He knew her name was Rita. He knew Spec 4 Doyle was protective enough of her to want to make sure his lieutenant understood that the girl always had been and always would be—irrepressible.

Which meant what? That she was his girlfriend, fiancée, ex-wife, cousin?

It didn't really matter—shouldn't really matter—but it did somehow. And that alone had given him cause for thought these past few days. Admittedly, she was a pretty woman—and she knew it. But there was more to it than that. *She* wasn't afraid to look him right in the eye, and if she was put off by his appearance or his helplessness, he certainly couldn't tell it. He'd never met a woman quite like her before. She was so…in control. She deliberately pushed his buttons, and she didn't care if he knew it. If anything, she dared him to do something about it.

And the problem was that he wanted to do something about it. He had spent an inordinate amount of time fantasizing about exactly what that would be. They had had two run-ins, both of them unpleasant. So how was it that, ever since, he'd felt better about his situation than he had in a long time? It didn't make any sense. The bottom line was that he wanted to see this woman again—sometimes more than he wanted to see Joanna.

He gave a quiet sigh. Poor Joanna. She felt sorry for him. And he felt sorry for her. What a great way to start a marriage.

He must have dozed, because when he opened his

eyes the room was dark. He made no effort to reach the light switch. He could hear music coming from across the hall. It wasn't loud. It was just… unacceptable. He didn't want to hear it. All he wanted was to be left alone. In silence. In darkness.

He closed his eyes again, searching for some kind of oblivion, however brief. But he couldn't go back to sleep, and he couldn't stand the musical intrusion. He slid to the edge of the bed and then to the floor, legs stiff, holding on to the bed until he could reach his walker. With the help of that contraption, he had been more or less ambulatory since the day he'd been abandoned without a wheelchair. He could suck up the pain and get around a little bit if he wanted to. And right now he wanted to.

He shuffled slowly, painfully, into the hall. There was no raucous laughter or anything that might indicate some kind of party, but he could still hear the music.

When he reached the partially closed door, he shoved it open without knocking. He expected— He didn't know what he expected. The room was empty except for her. Doyle's blonde sat in a chair in front of the window, her long legs draped over one of the arms and a boom box on the floor by her side.

"Turn that thing off," he said, in spite of how surprised he was to see her.

"Well, look at you," she said. "Walking—and not bleeding or…anything."

"I said, turn that thing off!"

She surprised him further by extending one long leg and kicking the off control with her foot. They stared at each other across the room, the sudden silence unnerving.

"Anything else?" she asked.

He didn't answer her. Instead, he dragged the walker around so he could go.

"Hey," she called when he had shuffled nearly out of the room. "You want a cold beer?"

"What—if I do?" he asked, looking over his shoulder. He was out of breath now, too out of breath to physically turn around.

"Then I've got one." She opened what he had thought was a big ugly—heavy—purse and pulled out a bottle, the ice still clinging to the sides.

"Just how much trouble are you looking for?" he asked.

"Oh, I don't know. How much have you got? Lighten up, Lieutenant. I brought this for Bugs, but I don't think he can have it."

"Where is Bugs?"

"He's gone to X ray. He's been there a long time. He's running a fever. They're a little bit worried about him. But you wouldn't know anything about that."

"I don't get out much," he said sarcastically.

"What? You couldn't ask?"

"Look—" he said, trying not to lose his temper any more than he already had.

"You really didn't know, did you? Got your own problems, right?"

"What the hell do you want from me!"

"What do I want? Let's see. You wouldn't happen to know anything about algebra, would you—"

He swore and shuffled the rest of the way out the door. And he didn't look back.

It was nearly dark when they finally returned Bugs to the room. Once again, he was surprised to see her, because Rita had been angry enough with him after his—whatever it was—on her behalf, not to come back to the hospital again. She didn't want him making apologies or excuses for her—ever— and most particularly not to McGraw. But after a day or so, she decided that he had probably summed up her entire personality in that one remark. She was, indeed, "Rita being Rita."

One of the nurses who helped return Bugs to his bed was apparently planning on staying, so Rita didn't tell him she'd had another adventure with his lieutenant. He looked so ill now, his eyes bright with fever, but he managed to smile when she surreptitiously revealed the cold beer. Unfortunately, it looked like he wouldn't have a chance to drink it.

"We're going to be busy here for a while," the nurse said. "If you want to, go ahead and say your goodbyes now. You can come back tomorrow."

"Okay," Rita said, giving Bugs a wink. "Looks

like they're throwing me out. I guess I'll...see you later.''

''Do me a favor, will you?'' he asked when she turned to leave.

''What?''

''You got a phone yet?''

''Yes.''

''Could you leave the number at the nurses' station? In case I want to tell you something or...'' He shrugged. ''Something.''

She looked at him, not understanding quite what he meant. She could leave her number right here and now—with him—just as easily.

But she didn't say that. If he wanted her phone number left at the nurses' station, she'd do it.

''You got it. Get some sleep, big guy,'' she said. ''You look like you need it.''

He managed another smile, briefly. ''Rita, I appreciate you coming by like you do. You know that. I ain't got no family here or nothing—''

''Hey, no problem.''

''Drive carefully,'' he said. ''Don't talk to strangers.''

She laughed and gave him a little wave as she closed the door, and she stood for a moment after she had stepped into the hall. Not talking to strangers would be hard to do. Her life was full of strangers. Olivia was still at the beach, and for all Rita knew, her own daughter might fall into the ''stanger'' category now, too. She didn't begrudge the time

Olivia was spending with her step-grandparents—or she tried not to. Grandparents were important; even she knew that. But there was nothing even remotely resembling a decent grandparent now on her side of the family, and Matt was an orphan. She wanted Olivia to have as much love as she could possibly get.

"Hey!" someone called, and she looked around. "Come here!"

The door to Lieutenant McGraw's room was open, but she made no attempt to go see what he wanted.

"Hey!" he said again. "Rita!"

This time she walked as far as the doorway. "Ms. Warren to you," she said, and if he hadn't caught himself in time, he would have actually smiled.

"Ms....Warren," he said after a moment. "I want to ask you something."

She made no attempt to invite him to do so.

"Could you come around where I can see you? This is killing my neck."

"Is that the question?" Rita asked.

"No, that's the prelude to the question. I'm not armed," he assured her, but she was still wary. She had no reason to think this would be anything but unpleasant.

"So what's the question?" she asked, stepping into the room. He was lying in bed again, on his stomach, and she moved to where he could see her without straining. "Change your mind about the beer?"

"No, I wanted to know what you meant—about the algebra."

"I didn't *mean* anything."

"Then why did you ask me if I knew anything about it? It was kind of a…strange question."

She looked at him and gave a quiet sigh. "I asked because I'm desperate."

"Desperate," he repeated.

"Yes, 'desperate.' I'm taking an algebra course—"

"*You're* taking an algebra course—"

"That's what I said—will you pay attention? I'm trying to get my G.E.D. I'm taking algebra. And I can't do the stuff. I don't understand it and I'm…desperate. If I'd mention it to *you,* I'd have to be, right?"

"Right," he agreed—to her surprise. "So can't you get the instructor to give you some extra help?"

"No, I can't. I used to know her—from when we were in high school together. It's hard enough being in her class. It would kill me to have her know I can't cut it," she said candidly. She suddenly smiled. "Of course, she's going to know sooner or later anyway—when I fail the stupid course."

He was looking at her intently—at her, not her legs.

"Okay," he said finally.

"Okay, what?"

"Okay, I know something about algebra. Actually, I know a lot. I could tutor you."

"If hell freezes over?" she suggested, far from convinced that he was serious.

"I don't care what the weather report is," he said. "I'm not going anywhere."

She began to look around the head of the bed.

"What are you looking for?" he asked.

"Morphine drip—there's got to be some explanation for this incredible offer."

"You're the one who asked. It's no big deal. I know algebra. I need something to do. Do you want help or don't you?"

"How much do you charge?"

"Depends."

"On what?"

"On how long you last."

"How long *I* last?"

"Hey, I'm not easy," he said.

"Well, me either," Rita assured him.

They stared at each other. He was the first to look away.

"So, is Bugs okay?" he asked, completely changing the subject.

"I don't know. He's still running a fever. Why are you doing this?" she asked bluntly. "Why would you want to help me?"

"I told you. I need something to do."

"Besides that."

"Let's just say it's because Bugs Doyle is a good soldier," he said.

She looked at him a moment longer, then walked toward the door.

"Okay," she said, abruptly turning back to him. "What time?"

"Nineteen hundred hours," he answered without hesitation—as if he'd worked out the particulars before he had even asked her.

She gave a little shrug. "Seven is good."

"Don't be late," he said.

"Get over yourself, McGraw," she told him as she went out the door. She kept smiling as she walked down the corridor, infinitely pleased that here just might be the possibility—however remote—that she could stay in the algebra class and not make a complete fool of herself. There must be a million people who could be teaching that class, but no. It just *had* to be someone who had always made Rita feel like the bastard at the wedding. When she walked in and saw "Bitsy" Corrin, now Welch, waiting, chalk in hand, it was as if Rita were back in high school again. Bitsy had been a charter member of the small but very exclusive teenage version of the "beautiful people," and all of Rita's insecurities about not belonging had come rushing back. But now—*now*—well, we'd just have to see.

At the last minute Rita remembered to stop by the nurses' station to leave her telephone number.

"I'll put this on his chart," the same nurse who

had invited her to leave said. "If he needs anything, we can call you, right?"

"Right. Can you tell me how he's doing?" Rita asked. "I mean, really."

"Well—the surgeon isn't thrilled about the fever this long after the initial injury. He's ordered some antibiotics intravenously. We'll just have to see."

Rita nodded and turned to go.

"Rita," the nurse called. "I…think I ought to tell you something."

"What?" Rita asked, alarmed because of her tone of voice.

"It's not about Bugs. It's about McGraw."

"What about him?"

"His mother found out about that little thing between you and him the other day. She's not happy."

"And?" Rita asked.

"And she's asked that you be barred from the unit—"

"What?" Rita said incredulously. "She can't do that—can she?"

"She runs with the big dogs. I don't think she can—but who knows? I just thought I'd tell you. She's supposed to be coming here tomorrow—and she'll probably be around for a few days. She's going to be hunting for bear. If I were you, I'd…stay out of her way."

"Thanks, but no thanks," Rita said. Her days of running from unpleasant situations were over.

"Rita, you're missing the point here."

"Which is?"

"If you get into some kind of…'discussion' with her, it's going to upset the whole unit. The men here don't need that kind of aggravation—especially McGraw. And our job is hard enough without having to referee."

"How am I supposed to see Bugs? Are you going to roll him down to the parking lot?"

"It's just for a few days. If he needs anything, he can call you—or I will. And I'll call you when the coast is clear."

"This isn't right. You know that," Rita said.

"Believe me, 'right' doesn't even enter into the equation. You do *not* want to tangle with her. Okay?"

"No, it's not okay! I can handle this."

"I'm sure you can. The question is how? *I* wanted to punch her in the nose, and I've got a lot more to lose than you have. It could get out of hand—"

"You don't have to worry about it."

"Rita—you're going to make me say this, aren't you? If you give her any trouble, she's going to go looking for reasons to keep you out of here—something besides talking back to her boy. Now, if she does that, don't you think she might find one or two little things you'd just as soon not be hauled out in plain view?"

Rita looked at her.

Imagine that, she thought sarcastically. Her "Ready Rita" reputation had preceded her, and this nurse believed every word of it.

"I was a dancer," Rita said evenly. "Period."

But she didn't wait to hear anything more. The woman was right. She wouldn't want McGraw's mother looking for reasons—not now when Rita was trying to get herself straightened out so she could be a part of Olivia's life again.

She walked hurriedly across the parking lot. The night was warm; she could feel the heat still rising from the pavement. But there was a storm coming. The wind had picked up and she could smell the rain not far off. She stood looking at the flashes of lightning on the southwestern horizon, wondering why everything was so hard. All she wanted was to see her baby, and here she was worried about Bugs, intimidated by a math teacher, and on the wrong side of a rich and influential woman she'd never even met. The only bright side of her whole day had been McGraw's unexpected offer to tutor her—and even that involved the danger of being hit with a magazine or a trash can.

She suddenly realized that she couldn't keep the seven o'clock algebra appointment with him—and worse, she couldn't tell him why.

She unlocked her car door and gave the bag with the beer a sling inside. Bugs had explained life's little ups and downs to her a long time ago—when she'd been so upset after Matt Beltran had married Corey.

Sometimes you eat the bear, baby—and sometimes the bear eats you.

And wasn't that the truth? She had been a whole lot better off doing high kicks and wearing beads and feathers.

Chapter Four

There was nothing like the cold light of day for regrets. McGraw lay in his usual facedown position all morning, wondering if—on top of everything else that was wrong with him—he had lost his mind. He didn't want to tutor anybody, for God's sake. He especially didn't want to tutor Doyle's blonde. He didn't want to be bothered with her, or her algebra, and by early afternoon he knew exactly what he would do about it. When she got here, he'd just have to tell her. He'd say he didn't feel up to it. She was a smart woman, despite her apparent lack of credentials and her misgivings about this class she was taking. He could put her off like that once or twice, and she'd get the hint, and if it happened to be a coward's way out on his part, then so be it.

The rest of the afternoon went by slowly, in spite of his having to go to therapy. He was tired when he finally returned to his room, and he slept for a while, waking with a start because of the onset of some dream he didn't quite remember and didn't want to.

And he didn't want to think about Doyle's blonde, either, in spite of the fact that he was still convinced that she was different from any other woman he'd ever met. He'd never known anyone so...genuine. She didn't have a high school diploma, and she wasn't ashamed to say so. She was trying to do something about it, and that was the part she focused on. He couldn't help but admire her willingness to get it done—even if it meant having to deal with him.

He looked at his watch. It was well past Rita Warren's E.T.A. He had slept through the evening meal. The tray was still sitting on the overbed table, close enough for him to reach it. He pulled it around, so that he could look at it.

Something over rice.

A lot of something over rice.

His healing process required more calories than someone as inactive as he was could possibly take in, but for once he was willing to make the effort, even if the menu included *this*.

He was just finishing the last of the mystery meat when one of the nursing staff came in, one of the "floaters," who showed up from time to time and whose name he had never bothered to learn. She glanced at the empty dishes, but made no comment. He supposed she would have heard that he was not receptive to positive reinforcement in the guise of being made a member of the Clean Plate Club.

"Do you need anything, Lieutenant?" she asked as she was about to take the tray away—probably in the event he felt inclined to throw things.

"No," he said. Then, "Yes. Did I...have any visitors while I was asleep?"

"Your mother called. I told you about it—she can't make it this weekend."

"I didn't mean her. I meant anyone else?" He made some effort to appear as if it didn't matter, but the very fact that he was asking lent some significance. He hadn't exactly been overrun with people eager to bask in the warm glow of his presence— and they both knew whose fault that was.

"No. No visitors."

"You're sure?"

"Who were you expecting?"

"Nobody," he said. "Forget it. Wait," he added when she was about to leave again. "Bugs Doyle. How is he doing?"

"He's...about the same," she said, and clearly she was wondering what this was all about. Lieutenant McGraw did not make conversation, either.

"Is that good or bad?"

"We're monitoring his condition."

"What the hell does that mean?"

"It means we're monitoring his condition. It also means he can't have visitors."

"None?"

"None."

"Not even his girlfriend."

"I don't know anything about a girlfriend, but it wouldn't matter. Whatever the doctor says goes. Usually," she added significantly. He got the point. His mother must have undone any number of doctors' orders by now.

"Anything else you want to know?" she asked.

"Well, if there is, I'm out of luck," he said. "Did you always know how to dance around questions like this, or did you have to learn?"

She smiled. "I had to learn. I'm good at it, too."

"Damn straight," he said as she carried the tray out. She was good—he'd give her that. But not as good as the old warhorse.

He looked at his watch and wondered if he dared to feel relieved. *Ms.* Warren was nearly an hour late. If he hadn't had any visitors, and Doyle couldn't have any, then that must mean that she wasn't going to show. He wouldn't have been surprised if she had planned to arrive well past the time he said for her to be here, just on general principles, but it was beginning to look as if he was off the hook. She wasn't trying to make some kind of statement by being late; she simply wasn't coming. This was better than he could have hoped for. He wouldn't have to make excuses. He was the one doing the favor here, and he could just forget the whole thing. If she didn't even bother to show or to let him know she wasn't coming, she couldn't possibly be surprised if he bailed out of the arrangement.

Outstanding, he thought. *Too easy.*

He lay there, listening. He could hear boisterous laughter somewhere down the hall—some of the men letting off steam or watching championship wrestling or beach bunny volleyball.

Or the latest rumblings of a war.

He smiled slightly to himself. Women and sports and war. Male icons if ever there were any.

But he couldn't hear anyone coming down the corridor in sexy high-heeled shoes no matter how hard he tried. He didn't want to, not really. He closed his eyes, but he wasn't sleepy. He felt far too agitated to sleep, in spite of his professed relief. He *was* relieved, damn it. He shouldn't have to keep reminding himself of that fact.

He thought about calling Joanna. He used to do that—call her for no reason whenever he got a chance, just to talk about nothing, just to hear her voice. He gave a quiet sigh. That was before she started looking like a deer caught in headlights all the time.

He abruptly reached for the telephone and dialed her number. It rang a long time, but no one answered. He tried once more, and then gave up. The last thing he needed was to lie in the dark and listen to the constant ringing of Joanna's unanswered phone.

But the day hadn't been a complete bust, he finally decided. His mother hadn't made it up from Savannah to visit. He loved her dearly, but she was nothing if not high maintenance. If she'd come today, they would have gone around and around again about his leaving the military and starting law school. She had never forgiven him for enlisting, never accepted his assertion that he had to do *something* that wasn't preordained.

Until that fateful day, when he aligned himself with the United States Army, he had kept the family traditions without question. He'd gone to the same prep school, the same college as all the McGraw males since the Civil War. But when it had come down to attending the same law school and joining the same firm, he just couldn't do it. He was from a long line of esteemed lawyers and judges, and he had spent years waiting—hoping—for some kind of genetic love-of-jurisprudence to kick in. It never did, and he'd finally had to do something about it. He had honestly thought that once he signed the dotted line, his mother would realize that any more discussion on the matter of his career choice would be useless. He couldn't have been more wrong.

Regardless of his mother's opinion, the army had been a lifesaver for him. As far as he was concerned, there was nothing like the military for getting one focused. He had understood the group dynamics from day one. His training had been especially designed to foster a curious but finely honed mix of rivalry and camaraderie, one that relentlessly propelled him not to fail either himself or the group. It had come as a surprise to him that he fit the army mold so well. He had a real aptitude for soldiering. He seemed to instinctively know what needed to be done, and he could communicate his self-assurance to other men. He liked the ordered discipline of military life. He liked the excitement and the adventure.

He had been on peacekeeping assignments all over the world, all of them dangerous, some more than others, but it wasn't until he was back here and on night training maneuvers that he'd ever been injured. The Black Hawk had gone down in the dark, and everyone on it had died except him and Bugs Doyle. By all logic, the two of them should be dead, too.

Mac didn't know if he had anything of his military career left, but he intended to hang on to it as long as he could. Maybe he was washed up. Maybe he'd never find the nerve to go up in an aircraft again—much less jump out of one, but his being hurt wasn't the godsend his mother had expected it to be. He still wasn't lawyer material, and he was just as hardheaded as she was. If she had driven up to see him today, sooner or later he would have said something to make her really angry. His poor mother. The only thing he'd done right as far as she was concerned was to become engaged to Joanna—and even that was in jeopardy.

Last but not least in his list of pluses, he really was off the hook with Doyle's blonde. Totally. Permanently.

And he was glad.

He was still glad the next morning and all during the afternoon and early evening, right up until nineteen hundred hours—when his gladness began to dissipate, only to be replaced by rampant annoyance.

No Ms. Warren.

When he couldn't stand it any longer, he went walking—shuffling—down the hall so he would be away from the room if she arrived. The last thing he wanted was for her to find him just sitting and waiting. He deliberately chose a direction where he could see the full length of the corridor and the elevators on his arduous return. Because it was the weekend, any number of people came and went—none of them her.

He walked some more, and he tried not to look as if he were interested in the elevator traffic. By the time he reached his room again, it was all too apparent that he had stayed on his feet too long. His knees were shaking with exhaustion, and the pain was excruciating. It was fortunate for Doyle's blonde that she didn't show. Given the state he was in, he might not have stopped with a magazine.

Eventually, when the burning in his legs had subsided somewhat, he called Joanna again. There was still no answer. He wondered idly where she could be, surprised by the fact that he was only curious and not jealous. But, if nothing else, hiking up and down the hall precipitated a good night's sleep, one without dreams of falling or burning or interacting with dead soldiers who were miraculously no longer dead. He woke on Sunday morning a wiser man and absolutely determined not to be jerked around again.

He didn't watch the clock or the door that evening, and he didn't do any reconnaissance up and down the hall. He made an attempt to find out about Doyle instead, and he was given the same non-answer: Doyle was being closely monitored.

But whatever their "monitoring" entailed, it still left them time to decide to put him into a wheelchair with his legs stretched out. He would have had to admit that that position didn't hurt as much as it used to, but he was out of sorts in spite of the improvement. He was so tired of everything and everybody. He hated the hospital and he hated that his only alternative was to throw in the towel and go home to Savannah. He therefore had no recourse but to sit by the window and feel sorry for himself— which he did with alacrity.

He was still feeling sorry for himself when he realized that he wasn't alone in the room. He looked around sharply, and there she stood, white sunglasses on top of her head, little pink dress and all, a textbook and a spiral composition book clutched to her breasts.

"Hi," she said.

"Where the hell have you been?" he asked, as if he had every right to ask that.

"Carolina Beach," she answered without hesitation.

"You went to the beach?"

"I did, yes."

"Did you forget you were supposed to be here?"

"I'm here now—"

"You were supposed to be here two damned days ago!"

"Why are you so upset? It's not like you were going anywhere—"

"I don't like being jerked around!"

She looked at him, but she didn't say anything.

"Well, I hope you had a good time," he said finally.

"It wasn't that kind of a trip."

"What kind was it?"

"Look, are we going to do this or not?" she asked.

"What kind was it?" he asked again, because knowing what she had been doing had suddenly become a priority.

She sighed. He waited.

"I had a problem," she said after a moment. "I told you before. You're not the only one—"

"What kind of problem?" He realized that he was stepping on all her responses, but he couldn't help it. He was more annoyed by her absence than he would ever have been willing to admit.

"The kind that made me do the same stupid thing I always do."

"Which is?"

"Run. Everybody's got their own way of trying to deal with stuff. You throw things and swear." She shrugged. "I run."

"To Carolina Beach?"

"Not always. This time I was looking for someone."

"Any luck?"

"Nope. I didn't know where to look." She sighed again. "I'm very sorry, Lieutenant McGraw, if I caused you any inconvenience. I didn't mean to."

She turned to go.

"Wait," he said. "Have you seen Bugs?"

"Yes," she said.

"You have?"

She smiled. "Sometimes, if you raise enough hell, you get what you want."

"I wouldn't know," he assured her.

"Well, not for lack of trying."

The remark was so well placed, he had to work at not losing his temper—or smiling.

"So, how is he?" he asked.

"He's still running a fever. He didn't have much to say."

"Maybe he was ticked off because you disappeared."

"No, he understands. Bugs always understands."

She said it with such conviction that he felt the sting of what could only be described as jealousy. He hadn't asked Doyle what his relationship with Rita Warren was, and perhaps he should have. He could ask *her,* of course. There was absolutely no reason at all why he couldn't—except that he thought she'd tell him.

They stared at each other.

"As long as you're here, we might as well do this," he said abruptly, because he was beginning to notice how pretty she looked. And how tired. It was…unsettling. Maybe she really did have a problem—other than wanting a fun weekend at the beach.

"You think?" she asked, teasing him again.

"Yeah, I think. Pull up a chair."

It took a bit of doing to work out the logistics of getting her close enough to see and not jar the wheelchair or his outstretched legs.

"Did you have an assignment?" he asked.

"It's on page ten," she said, leaning closer. She picked up the book and began to hunt through it, finding the right place and turning it so he could see. "So how come you can tutor algebra?"

"I used to do it before I got hurt. High school and middle school kids. It was part of a community service program for troubled kids and P.R. for the military kind of thing."

She looked at him doubtfully—as if she couldn't

reconcile what she knew of him with the suggestion that he might have had a social conscience, but she didn't comment. He could just detect the scent of her perfume. No, it wasn't perfume at all. It was that same pleasant almond-and-cherry-scented soap or lotion or whatever it was. He had found it affecting before; it was incredible this close—light and heady all at the same time. Her arms were bare, and her skin looked soft and inviting. He could easily imagine how it would feel to touch her, and if he pressed his face against her neck...

He abruptly took the book and tried to concentrate on the page she showed him.

"Did you do any of the problems?"

"No," she said. "Yes."

He gave her a look.

"Yes, because I made the attempt," she said. "No, because I didn't know what I was doing."

"Let me see."

She opened the notebook and showed him. He recognized immediately that she had certainly told the truth regarding her math skills. She didn't understand the first thing about the process.

And he was not entirely unhappy with the realization that teaching her was going to take some time.

Rita lay awake in the dark, listening to the rain. She could hear the wind sighing in the pines. She had always loved that sound, even when she was a little girl. It was one of the few pleasant things in her childhood still worth remembering. The pines in a rainstorm. Whippoorwills on a hot summer night. Violets growing by her grandmother's back steps.

She was tired, but she couldn't get to sleep. She kept thinking about McGraw. For someone who was so notoriously ill-tempered, his patience as a tutor surprised her. The man was a magazine-thrower. A swearer and a trash can-tosser. The man also knew his algebra.

He'd had more than one opportunity to put her in her place this evening, to show her just how incredibly stupid she was, but he hadn't done it. He was all business, of course, meticulously explaining the principles of "unknown quantities" and the definition of "distributive properties." There was nothing about his demeanor that invited idle conversation. He wrote down number after number, letter after letter, equation after equation. He even drew pictures, and only once did he thump her on the head with a pencil.

She smiled in the darkness. She had deserved it, because her attention had wandered. But it wasn't because she had become bored with his efforts or because she didn't want to learn. It was because of the look on the nurse's face when she walked by the open doorway and saw Rita and Lieutenant McGraw sitting together.

Engaged Lieutenant McGraw.

Lieutenant McGraw with the powerful and rich

mother who had already ordered Rita Warren off the unit.

She supposed that his mother would have had very much the same expression on her face if she'd walked by—only she wouldn't have gone on about her business. *She* would have called the M.P.'s.

McGraw didn't notice the nurse at all, only that Rita wasn't listening to him. She would have liked to have asked how his visit with his mother had gone this weekend, but she hadn't—he had that pencil and he wasn't afraid to use it.

The woman must not have mentioned her displeasure with Rita Warren—or he wouldn't have agreed to tutor her. Or maybe she had mentioned it and he'd decided to do the tutoring anyway, just to annoy her. Bugs had said they were known to butt heads, and if McGraw wanted to rattle his mother's cage, Rita couldn't think of a better way to do it.

She sighed quietly in the dark. She hadn't quite told McGraw the truth. She hadn't been running away when she'd gone to Carolina Beach. She'd been running *toward*. She had suddenly wanted to see Olivia so badly, even if it was just to catch a glimpse of her. She had impulsively jumped in the car and headed east, and she'd driven up and down the streets of the town, walked up and down the beach itself for nearly two days looking for her. She wanted to feel those little arms around her neck again, smell her sweet baby smell. She kept imagining Olivia building sand castles or letting the waves chase her back and forth in the sunshine or looking for seashells. Happy, but not as happy as she'd be when she looked up and saw her real mother.

But real life wasn't like the movies. At least not in her case. Most of the time she felt like a bit player in her own life story, never the star, never the one who finally got the happily-ever-after kind of ending. In a movie, she would have found Olivia, and they would have had a wonderful reunion as the waves crashed and the seagulls flew. No, better than that. *She'd* be married to Matt Beltran now and they'd all be a family.

She sighed again. She couldn't hold on to that fantasy anymore, no matter how hard she tried. There was one little detail that kept getting in her way.

Reality.

Matt Beltran loved his wife.

Rita didn't want to be married to a man who not only didn't love her but was deeply in love with someone else. She had way too much pride for that, and she by no means thought he'd just wake up one morning and see the error of his ways. Basically what she wanted was a marriage *like* his and Corey's. She wanted a relationship with a man she absolutely knew would be there for her, no matter what.

She had no idea what she needed to do now. As far as she could tell, there was nothing to be done— except wait and maybe learn algebra. The hour she'd spent with McGraw had helped with that at least. She was no Einstein as yet, but she was definitely less bewildered. Now, if she could just remember what she'd learned until she got to class again.

She closed her eyes and willed herself to sleep. She wouldn't be tutored again until Wednesday, but she had plenty to do in the meantime. As Bugs had pointed out to her when she'd told him about her ill-conceived beach trip, Operation Olivia was still in full swing. She had to get herself gainfully employed, and she had no time to concern herself about McGraw.

Chapter Five

"Don't look at me," McGraw said. And he meant it.

"Why not?"

"I don't like it."

"I have to look at you. I can't concentrate on what you're telling me if I don't."

"Look at the page," he said, because he was the one who couldn't concentrate. "I mean it!"

"All right!"

She dutifully looked down at the page, but this was their fourth session and he knew her well enough now to recognize that she wasn't going to do it for long.

"It's not that bad," she said after a moment, eyes still averted.

"What are you talking about?"

"I'm talking about what you're talking about."

"Which is?"

"Your face. You don't want me to look at you because you're self-conscious about it—and there's no reason to be."

"You think they hid all the mirrors from me and I don't know what I look like?"

"No, I think you're giving up way too soon. You're a little crisp around the edges, McGraw, but I'm telling you, it's going to be all right. You're already past the 'bad sunburn' phase and then—"

"I guess you know more about it than I do," he said sarcastically. "More than the doctors, too."

"Well, I've known guys who were hurt—burned—like you and Bugs," she said, looking at him again in spite of what he'd said. "Your face won't be exactly the same. You're going to have that one place on your cheek, but it's not going to be all that bad. You aren't going to scare dogs and little children—well, you might, but it won't be because of the way you look."

He didn't say anything.

"Oh, right. You don't care about dogs and little children. Okay, then—Joanna isn't going to want to put a paper bag over your head every time the two of you go out to dinner. You're still going to be a babe. Trust me."

He ignored the "babe" remark. "What do *you* know about Joanna?"

"Nothing," she said airily.

"Did she say something to you?"

"Not about the way you looked," Rita assured him.

She was trying to jerk him around—again, and he absolutely was not going to let her. When he didn't say anything else, she made a great show of turning her attention back to the page.

"You pretty boy heartthrobs are all alike," she said not quite under her breath, and he took the bait, just as she likely had known he would.

"What is that supposed to mean?"

"You *are* more than your face, aren't you, Lieutenant? Or did Mama and Daddy have to send you for therapy every time you got a zit?"

"Very funny."

"I'm just saying—"

"Do the math, will you!"

"Get over yourself, McGraw. I *was* doing it. You're the one who interrupted the process here. Check this out." She pushed the sheet of paper she'd been working so hard on toward him.

He took it and began looking for mistakes in her problem solving.

"Well?" she asked pointedly.

"It's…correct."

"Yes! And it killed you to say so, didn't it? I'm doing good, right?"

"You're doing okay."

"Okay enough to close up shop a little early?"

"Yeah, why not?" he said, surprised that he was more than a little miffed by the unexpected request. Not that he didn't know it was purely a token one. She'd go if she wanted to, no matter what he said.

"Great!" she said, slamming the book closed.

"Got a big night planned?" he asked in spite of everything he could do.

"Got a date with a real angel!" she called over her shoulder as she disappeared into the hall. "See you tomorrow!"

"Eighteen-hundred!" he yelled, changing the time just to feel like he had some control in the matter.

"Okay!" he heard her yell back—which must have thrilled the medical staff.

He sat watching the empty doorway, amazed by his level of aggravation. And there was no legitimate reason for it. She had been showing up on time and she was doing well. There was no reason why she couldn't end this evening's session early if she wanted to. There was no money changing hands, and her leaving made no difference to him one way or the other. He certainly didn't care. He could always...

He gave a sharp sigh. He just didn't like being uninformed. If she was supposed to belong to Doyle, then what was she doing going out with somebody else? And what kind of guy would be described like that—an "angel"? Somebody nonmilitary and without broken bones and burns, he supposed.

Or maybe he had jumped to the wrong conclusion. Maybe Doyle was the angel. Maybe they had something special planned here in the hospital. Doyle was better. He could have visitors now—not that the "no visitor" thing had ever stopped Rita. McGraw tried to imagine Joanna bucking the system like that and couldn't. His mother, yes. Joanna, no. Joanna had canceled on him twice of late. She couldn't make the three-and-a-half hour drive from Savannah to Fayetteville. She had a migraine. She had to work late. He wasn't fooled. Something was going on with her, and he didn't have the guts to ask what.

He looked up at a commotion in the hallway. A contingent of restless soldier-patients, moving along en masse, some hobbling, some in wheelchairs, and all of them on an impromptu quest for entertainment.

Bugs Doyle rode happily along right in the middle of them.

"She's asleep, Rita."

"I got here as soon as I could. I thought you said they'd be here sometime after seven—" She broke off. There was no point in arguing. "Olivia was pretty tired, I guess."

Matt didn't answer her. She could see Corey come to stand behind him. She looked tanned and rested, and she was holding the little prince, who seemed glad to have company if no one else did. He kept grinning from ear to ear—unlike his father.

"Rita," Corey said after a moment. "Why don't you come in? There's no reason why you can't see her even if she is asleep."

Rita looked at her gratefully, but she didn't voice her gratitude. It would have been too much to have to thank Corey for letting her see her own child.

"Her room is still in the same place," Corey said.

Rita could feel Matt's resistance to her being here, but she didn't hesitate. She went down the hall to the small room where Olivia lay sleeping. The room was pretty much the way she remembered it. New paint, maybe. And a teddy bear wallpaper border that Olivia must love. It had been put down low where Olivia could see it. Rita had the sudden mental image of Matt and Corey doing this together for "their" baby girl.

Olivia wasn't in a crib anymore. She was in one of those low, molded plastic things that looked like anything except what it was. A castle? No, a cottage with a fence. She glanced around the room. There was a kind of child-size coatrack thing in the corner, but instead of coats there were any number of hats, some with flowers, some with bows, some with flowers *and* bows. Rita smiled to herself. Her baby always did like hats.

Olivia slept soundly, one little foot out from under the cover. There was a white rocking chair in the room, and Rita pulled it closer to the bed. She sat quietly. It was all she could do not to touch her sleeping child. Olivia wasn't the way Rita remembered. In the months that had passed since their last visit, Olivia had changed from a chubby walking baby into a little girl.

Rita sat there for a long time, and she would have sat longer if Corey hadn't come to the door.

"Want some ice tea?" Corey asked.

Rita tried to find some reason to be offended by the question, but she couldn't. Corey hadn't asked her to *leave*. She'd asked if she were thirsty.

"Yeah, okay," Rita whispered, getting out of the rocking chair. She gave Olivia one last look before she followed Corey down the hall and into the kitchen.

Matt and the little prince were nowhere to be seen. Rita stood for a moment then sat at the kitchen table.

"Thanks," she said when Corey handed her the glass. She took a sip. Naturally, it was sweet and lemony and good. Everything Corey did was good.

"Matt says you're staying for a while," Corey said, sitting with her own glass.

Here it comes, Rita thought. The fishing expedition.

"I'm thinking of starting a business," she said, watching Corey closely for signs of disbelief.

"What kind of business?" Corey asked right on cue. So far, she was doing all right with her face.

"Aerobics classes," Rita said. She gave a slight

smile. "Las Vegas style. I learned a lot about the right way to dance—so you don't overexert yourself and pull muscles and stuff. I told Bugs I might as well use it."

"Well, that sounds workable to me," Corey said.

"You think so?"

"Sure. People get tired of the same old exercise classes. I think what you're talking about would be...unusual enough to make it interesting. Kind of like belly dancing."

"Exactly. I'm still looking for a place to rent— it's got to be big enough for people to parade back and forth—" She suddenly stopped. She didn't want to talk about this. Corey Beltran *always* had that kind of effect on her. The woman was so comfortable or something. They'd hardly gotten past hello and here Rita was just a hair away from blurting out how much she didn't want to go back to dancing in one of the boulevard clubs—and how afraid she was that she might have to.

"Is Olivia all right?" Rita asked abruptly.

"Yes."

"Does she ever—" Rita stopped again. She couldn't bring herself to ask.

"What?" Corey asked after a moment.

"Okay. I want to know if she ever calls you 'Mama.'"

"No, she calls me 'Corey.'"

"I guess people wonder about that."

"Well, if they do, they don't say so."

"Do you think Olivia is going to know who I am?"

"It's…hard to say."

"What do you mean, it's hard to say?" Rita asked, alarmed by even the vague suggestion that what she feared the most might be true.

"Sometimes she's shy."

"With strangers, you mean."

"Rita, she hasn't seen you for a long time."

"You showed her the pictures I sent, didn't you?"

"Yes. I told you I did. In the last letter I sent."

"I know, I know. I just—" Rita gave a quiet sigh. There was no point in starting something with Corey. It was the old Rita who always lashed out at the nearest warm body whenever things weren't going her way. She had enough sense to know that she didn't want to alienate either Corey or Matt, and if anyone had ever treated her decently when she had no reason whatsoever to do so, it was Corey Beltran.

"I…appreciated all the progress reports and the pictures and everything," she said. It took some effort on her part to do it, but she managed to get the words out.

Corey nodded. "So, how is Bugs?"

"He's—" Rita started. Then, "Why are you asking?"

"I thought you were going to the hospital to see him."

"Now how would you know that—you've been at the beach for weeks."

Corey smiled. "The sergeant told me."

"The sergeant doesn't miss much, does he?" Rita asked, wondering why she was surprised to know that Matt had checked to see if she had done what he asked—or more likely, to see if she'd kept her word.

"No, not much," Corey said. "And Lou said she saw you."

"What did she do? Make a special trip to tell you trouble was back in town?"

"Pretty much," Corey answered in that truthful way she had, and Rita couldn't help but smile.

But the smile faded. "I'm going to want to see my baby, Corey."

"So come to supper tomorrow," Corey said without hesitation.

"Supper—me?"

"Yes, you. Six o'clock. Plan to stay and visit with Olivia afterward."

The old Rita stared at her, trying to see the ulterior motive in the invitation.

"Or not," Corey said when the silence went on too long.

"No. No, I'll be here. I was just…surprised."

"You have visitation rights, Rita. You shouldn't be."

"Yeah, well," Rita said, still not sure. "Does

Matt know, or are you going to have to play 'Guess Who's Coming To Dinner' after I leave?''

"He knows. Olivia is the most important thing here."

Rita didn't say anything, but she understood the intent behind the remark. The Beltrans were going to try to get along with her, and she would be welcome as long as she behaved in a way that didn't upset Olivia—visitation rights or not, real mother or not.

She tried to be angry and couldn't quite get there. *I must be getting better at this,* she thought. "Okay, then. Should I bring anything?"

"Just yourself."

"Six o'clock?"

"Right. If Matt doesn't get home by then, we'll start without him—well, look who's here," Corey said, smiling. "Come on. It's okay—"

Rita looked around. Olivia hesitated in the doorway, her finger in her mouth, her eyes heavy with sleep and her chubby little legs sticking out from under her pink-and-white nightie. When she came forward, Rita started to reach for her, but Olivia hadn't even noticed her presence. She went straight for Corey.

"Where's Poppy?" she asked sleepily, climbing into Corey's lap.

"Poppy's at his house," Corey said. "You remember. We took Poppy and Nana home."

"Let's go see Poppy. Let's go see Nana—"

"Olivia?" Rita said, because she couldn't stay on the sidelines any longer. "Olivia, baby, it's me—it's Mama—"

Olivia looked at her for a moment then turned back to Corey. "Let's go see Poppy," she said. "He needs a story."

"I tell you what. You can call Poppy and Nana on the telephone tomorrow. Right now it's time for little girls to go to sleep."

"No, Co-wee…"

"Yes, Olivia," Corey said, smiling. "I tell you what *else*. Maybe Mama needs a story—"

"No," Olivia said, getting down from Corey's lap. "Not Mama."

She walked right past Rita's outstretched hand and disappeared into the hallway. Corey got up to follow her. She seemed about to say something, then didn't. What was there to say? Clearly Olivia wasn't interested in her so-called real mother.

"Rita, I'm sorry…" Corey began when she came back.

"Are you?" Rita asked, trying not to cry. That was the last thing she wanted to do. *Cry*. It wasn't as if she hadn't expected Olivia's indifference. It wasn't as if she didn't deserve it.

"Olivia is just tired from the trip home. Come to supper tomorrow, okay?"

Rita didn't say anything. She got up from the chair and walked toward the back door.

"Okay," she said when she reached it, but she

didn't stop. She had to get out of here. She ran into Matt on the porch steps. He was carrying that still happy baby boy. She could see the old man who lived across the street waving to them as he went back into his house.

She pushed on past Matt without saying a word.

"Now what?" she heard him ask Corey.

Her phone was ringing when she got home. She could hear it when she opened the front door. She was in no hurry to answer it, but it didn't stop. Finally she picked up the receiver.

"How did it go?" Bugs asked.

She gave a quiet sigh.

"That bad," he said.

"Olivia…didn't want anything to do with me."

"Well, she'll have to get used to you, won't she? You have to give it time—"

"I don't want to give it time. She's *my* baby."

"And Beltran's. You're not going to do anything crazy, are you? I thought you had all this straight now."

"I do," she said after a moment. "It's just…hard, you know?"

"You're not crying, are you?"

"No," she said, but it wasn't quite the truth and he knew it.

"Don't do that, baby," he said. "It's not going to help a—"

He didn't say anything else.

"Bugs?" she said.

"Yeah, I'm here. The lieutenant was at the door. I thought he wanted something—but he's off walking again. First they can't get him to walk, now they can't get him to stop."

"Can you tell him something?"

"What?"

"Can you tell him I can't do the algebra thing tomorrow—"

"No, you'd better do that."

"Why? He's right there."

"He's not *right* here. But if he was, it's not something I ought to be doing."

"Why?"

"Rita, trust me on this, will you? I'm too far down on the totem pole to be telling him something that's got to do with his personal life."

"Tutoring algebra isn't personal, Bugs. My guess is that he thinks it's more like a plague from the bowels of hell," she said, because she thought McGraw wouldn't do it all if he didn't feel some kind of guilty obligation to the only other survivor of the helicopter crash.

"Well, whatever it is, it ain't army business. Besides that, I think he's upset about something again. Call the desk and have one of the nurses tell him, okay?"

She sighed instead of answering.

"Rita? You ain't mad, are you?"

"Bugs, how could I be mad at you? I'm glad you called, okay?" she added after a moment.

"What are friends for?"

"Well, not for carrying messages, that's for sure," she said, and he laughed.

"Don't worry about Olivia, okay? It's going to work out— Hey, wait a minute, wait a minute," he said when she was about to hang up. "One of the nurses just came in. Here—tell her to tell the lieutenant you're bailing out tomorrow."

"I'm not bailing out. I'm going to see—"

"Hello?" a woman said, and Rita gave up in exasperation.

"Hi," she said to whatever unsuspecting bystander Bugs had handed the phone. "This is Rita Warren. I was wondering if you would tell Lieutenant McGraw something. Would you tell him I can't make it tomorrow?"

"Sure, I'll tell him."

"Thanks," Rita said. "And tell Bugs thanks, too," she said with a facetiousness that would be lost on the woman.

Rita hung up the phone, her mind already deep into "worst-case scenarios" about tomorrow. What if she and Olivia never got past this? What if Olivia never loved her again?

She looked around the room. The place was nice enough, maybe too nice for someone like her. After a moment she did what she always did when she was worried and upset. It had worked when she was twelve years old. It had worked when she was nineteen. And it worked now.

She turned on the radio, cranked the music up loud and began to dance.

Chapter Six

"Who's that?" Rita asked.

"P'Pan."

"P'Pan?"

"Yes."

"You like him?"

"Yes. He fies."

"He *does?* Cool. And who's that?"

"Tink-a-bell," Olivia said. "And John and Michael…and…Wendy," she added, pointing to each of them on the rumpled page of the Peter Pan book. Clearly, Olivia had already grasped the situation. This Mama person was here again, and she didn't know a thing.

"And Nana Dog!" Olivia concluded.

"Not to be confused with Nana, my mother," Corey said, smiling. "Okay, ladies, supper's ready."

"Wash the hands!" Olivia said, grabbing Rita's hand and trying to pull her up from the couch.

"Sing the A-B-C song while you suds up," Corey said in passing.

The hand washing was a rousing success, if Rita did say so herself, and probably because of the tip Corey gave her on the way out. Olivia could really rock to the A-B-C ditty. Rita was still smiling when she sat at the table.

Matt had to stay late on the post—what a surprise—so the meal—chicken pot pie—was women and children only. At one point, Rita took the little prince and held him while Corey went to answer the phone. She was immediately awash in a flood of memories of Olivia at that age, memories of the love she had felt for her baby girl and the overwhelming fear that came from being all alone and not knowing what to do and not having anyone to ask. She had been so determined to make it by herself. She had resolved early on not to ever tell Matt Beltran about the baby they had made.

If the circumstances had been different, she might have. If he'd cared about her a little, or if he'd remembered the one and only night they had been together. He didn't—*still* didn't—but he took the responsibility for his daughter anyway. Rita had deliberately taken advantage of him the night Olivia was conceived. She took advantage of his grief and his guilt and vulnerability, because she cared about him, and she had tried to comfort him the only way she could. Her darling Olivia was the result. It was only when she couldn't make it any longer that she'd involved Matt. She'd lost her job. She'd been evicted, locked out of the place she was renting, and the sleazy landlord, rebuffed in his efforts to arrange "another way" for Rita to pay him, had confiscated everything inside.

Rita could do nothing about it. She had no money. She had nothing, except a hungry and homeless, unkempt child. Thinking back now about the shape Olivia had been in when she'd left her on the military base in Matt's car, Rita felt nothing but shame. She simply hadn't known what else to do, and the truth of the matter was that there was nobody in the world she could trust to take care of her baby but Matt. She didn't know much about government agencies, and what she did know hardly recommended them. She thought they'd whisk Olivia away to a foster home—which they did, of course. But she *knew* Matt Beltran would do the right thing for Olivia, and he had. Olivia was happy now, just as Rita had wanted. There was nothing wrong with the final outcome. She recognized that the choices she'd made were wrong. Desperate or not, overwhelmed or not, she shouldn't have abandoned her child.

The baby boy bounced up and down on Rita's lap.

"What's this baby's name, Olivia?" she asked.

"Brother," Olivia said promptly.

"No, his other name."

"Robot Jays."

"Robert James?"

"Uh-*huh!*" Olivia said, clapping her hands.

"Well," Rita said, lifting him up and turning him around where she could see his happy little face. "Bobby-Jim, how in the world are you?"

The baby giggled, and so did Olivia.

Corey returned, and the rest of the meal went well enough. In fact, the entire evening went well. With Corey's permission, Rita gave Olivia her bath and put her to bed, and she left the Beltran house hopeful, if not entirely elated. Once Olivia's initial shyness had dissipated, she seemed happy enough to have Rita there—but it was obvious which of the two women she considered her "mother," and that was probably the reason Corey had been so willing to let Rita come again—if she called first. Even so, it was a concession Rita was willing to make.

Rita slept fitfully, finally falling into a deep sleep when it was time to get up again. She toyed seriously with the idea of forgetting about her date with Mrs. Corrin-Welch and the community college algebra class, and it took a great deal of willpower on her part to roll out of bed. She arrived for her adventure into the wonderful world of mathematics cranky and sleep-deprived and generally out of sorts. Mrs. Corrin-Welch greeted them all with that dreaded command, "Get out a blank sheet of paper."

The unexpected test was difficult, and Rita had to work hard not to panic. She calculated and recalculated, and all the while she hung on to McGraw's algebra axiom for dear life.

It's only numbers.

It's only numbers.

And letters. And "properties." And...

Oh, God.

Rita was the last one to hand in her test paper.

"Bitsy?" she said as she laid the sheet of paper on the desk, and she realized the moment she used Mrs. Corrin-Welch's old high school nickname, that she had been feeling inferior and intimidated for nothing. Dear old "Bitsy," her former classmate, now algebra instructor, didn't even remember her. The woman had had no idea that Rita Warren, third from the front, second row, had a place, albeit insignificant, in her personal history.

"I was wondering if you'd grade this now," Rita said anyway.

"Well, I—" Bitsy looked up at her, and clearly she was still trying to decide how Rita could know the name that was so indicative of her glory days.

"It's important," Rita said, and it was precisely because Bitsy didn't remember who Rita was that she complied.

Bitsy abruptly gave a small token smile and began to look over the test paper, red pencil in hand.

"You missed one," she said after a moment.

"One?" Rita said incredulously. "Are you sure?"

"Yes, of course. You did very well."

"Could I have it back? I want to show it off."

"Well—"

"It's important. Really important."

"Just bring it to the next class. We're going to go over all of the—"

"Right! The next class," Rita said, grabbing it up. She had to show McGraw this. He'd never believe it if she just *told* him. *She* didn't believe it, even with the proof in her hand.

Rita waited until the early afternoon to drive to the hospital, just missing an empty space on her first search through the parking lot. She finally found one some distance from the hospital entrance, one too small for a less adventurous driver, because both neighbors had parked on the dividing lines. She managed to squeeze in, and when she was about to make an attempt to get out of the car, she saw McGraw's fiancée, Joanna, hurrying to a silver, semiconvertible, T-top something, one row over.

She wouldn't have noticed her at all, if she hadn't been more or less running, and she continued to watch as Joanna got into the car on the passenger side. There was a man in the driver's seat; Rita could see him plainly. She had to walk right past them to get to the nearest sidewalk. When she was nearly even with the car, the man took Joanna into his arms and held her, then, as Rita watched, riveted, he kissed her. And this was no brother, cousin or only-a-friend, peck-on-the-cheek kind of kiss. This was the real thing.

Rita kept walking. When she crossed in front of the car, she turned to look back at just the moment Joanna saw her through the windshield.

Busted, Rita thought, because there was no doubt in her mind that Joanna had recognized her. The woman was obviously upset, but whether she'd been in that state before she got into the car or whether it was the result of having been seen, Rita couldn't begin to guess. And she didn't want to. This was none of *her* business, and there was no reason why she should be feeling so indignant on McGraw's behalf. If McGraw thought he was engaged, well, then, that was *his* problem. Who was she to point out a pothole on the road to wedded bliss—huge though it may be? Maybe it wasn't what it looked like. Maybe the whole thing was completely innocent. Maybe there was a reasonable explanation, like…Joanna had something in her eye.

And maybe Rita should go buy herself a pair of binoculars so she wouldn't miss all those pigs when they started flying.

Shame on you, Rita admonished herself silently as she deliberately gave Joanna a friendly wave. Let Joanna worry about whether or not Rita had seen anything. Let her worry about whether or not Rita would go right now and tell McGraw all about it.

Rita continued walking toward the hospital entrance, half expecting Joanna to leap out of the car and run after her. But she didn't, and Rita understood perfectly. People believed whatever they needed to believe, and right now Miss Joanna needed to believe that Rita couldn't see past the nose on her face.

Or she wanted Rita to be the one to break the news to McGraw that his engagement was in serious trouble here. She was still reviewing the possibilities when she got off the elevator on his floor, and still perplexed enough to go by and see Bugs first.

He wasn't in the room, which was just as well. She might not have been able to keep from verifying his suspicion that his lieutenant was having fiancée troubles, even when she knew she shouldn't. It was just that the whole scenario had been such a surprise. She had met the lovely Joanna, and the girl did *not* seem like the type to cheat on the man she was supposed to marry. And even if she was, as Bugs had put it—McGraw's mama was rich. And Mc-Graw wasn't half bad himself, regardless of recent traumatic events. All that would be hard to throw aside, to Rita's way of thinking. Of course, his personality needed a little fine tuning and he was in the army—for the moment, anyway—and Rita supposed that that could be a definite downside for some.

She walked across the hall to McGraw's room.

He wasn't in, either, so she left and went in the direction of the day room to search for one or the other of them, preferably McGraw. That test paper was burning a hole in her pocket. She wanted him to see it. And be impressed. And not think she was so dumb after all. She'd been on a roll of late, and she wanted to keep it going, if at all possible. She'd had a good visit with Olivia. She'd passed her algebra test. And now she wanted to show off for McGraw.

She found him finally, standing at the end of the corridor. She noticed immediately that he'd advanced from a walker to a pair of crutches. Not that he was using them at the moment for anything except to keep his balance. He was just...standing, staring out the window. He didn't look around when she walked up.

"Hi," she said after a moment.

"What are you doing here?" he asked without looking at her.

"I came to tell you something—"

"Not interested," he said, cutting her off.

She wanted to see what he was looking at so intently, and she moved closer. From this vantage point he had an excellent view of the parking lot. The silver something was still sitting in the same place, and McGraw could see directly into it. Had he been standing here for the clench? If he had, then he must have seen Rita, too, and now he must be thinking that she'd come to give him the good news about his fiancée—or to gloat.

"I passed the test," she said abruptly.

He finally looked at her. "What?"

"An algebra test. A pop quiz. I passed it. No, I didn't just 'pass' it. I aced it. Here, see?"

She pulled the test paper out of her pocket and unfolded it so he could get the full effect of the big, red "95" in the upper right corner. He did look at it, but it might as well have been written in Egyptian hieroglyphs as far as he was concerned.

The heck with this, Rita thought.

"McGraw, are you okay?" she asked bluntly.

He glanced at her. "I'm...tired," he said.

"Then *sit down* somewhere. You want me to find you a wheelchair?"

"No, I want you to leave me the hell alone."

"You got it, Lieutenant," she said, turning to go.

"No, wait," he said. He reached out to keep her there. One crutch fell forward, and she had to catch it to keep it from clattering to the floor.

"I'm...sorry. I—it's this place. I'm just so damned tired of it. I need to get out of here. I need to..."

What? Rita thought. *Hobble down to the parking lot and kick some butt?*

She looked out the window again. Joanna and her "friend" were gone. Rita folded the test paper and put it back into her pocket.

"Okay," she said. "Go put your pants on. I'll be right back."

"Wait!" he called after her. "What are you going to do?"

"You want out, we're going to get it done. See the hill and so forth, Lieutenant McGraw," she called.

It took her longer than she expected—a *no* would have been much quicker. A *yes* involved all kinds of discussion and paperwork.

"He has to stay out of the sun," the physician on call told her.

"Right," Rita said.

"And don't let him get drunk."

"I beg your pardon—"

"He's heard about the beer you brought Bugs," one of the nurses said.

"He didn't *drink* it," Rita said. "Knowing that he possibly could have is what counted. People have to feel like they're a little in control."

"Which is why I'm going to let Lieutenant McGraw go out for a while. I'm not sure your company is going to be any less aggravating than his mother's, but the mere fact that he's finally expressed an interest in *something* is enough to get my vote."

Rita tried to look as if she agreed, and that his remark about her being aggravating didn't offend her.

"Try not to throw any magazines at each other, okay? Enjoy," he said, handing her a slip of paper.

"What is this?"

"*That* is just in case post security thinks you two look as suspicious as I do."

"I don't know *what* you're talking about," Rita assured him, but she didn't wait around for an explanation.

She found McGraw pretty much the same as when she'd left him—only sitting. And he apparently didn't have any pants—or if he did, he wasn't about to put them on and have her think for one minute that he believed that she could really get him out of the hospital.

Which made the look on his face all the sweeter when she told him.

"You're kidding," he said.

"Nope. Here it is," she said, holding up the slip of paper between her fingers. "You're out of here until 9:00 p.m. Unless you've changed your mind, of course."

"Hell, no," he said, struggling to get up. "Let's go."

"Hold it! Your doctor seems to think one of us might look like he's trying to go AWOL. Call me peculiar, Lieutenant, but I don't much want to be seen with you in your bathrobe and your underwear. I can live with the bandages, but don't you have a...physical training ensemble or something?"

"I'm wearing the P.T. ensemble," he said, showing his genuine army-issue, run-the-eight-minute-mile-at-some-ungodly-hour shorts and T-shirt.

"Then lose the robe. And don't start with me, McGraw—I have an image to maintain here. How well can you hobble these days?"

"Well enough."

"Good. I'm going to go get the car. If you head out right now, maybe you'll get to the front door by midnight."

"You just be sure you've got the car door open and the motor running."

She didn't have to wait for him. One of the staff had loaded McGraw into a wheelchair and delivered him promptly to the front door. She had already slid the front seat on the passenger side back as far as it would go, so his getting into the car wasn't as difficult as one might have thought, once they found a place to stow the crutches.

She didn't ask him where he wanted to go. She didn't ask him anything. All she knew was that she wasn't about to mention seeing Joanna kissing somebody in the parking lot, and clearly, neither was he.

He must have seen her, she kept thinking. Or else he wouldn't be so upset, and he wouldn't have come on this jaunt with her. And he *was* upset. The fact that he was trying so hard not to show it told her that.

"Just so you know," she said as she took the exit

to head north on the interstate. "We are *not* listening to country-western music."

He glanced at her, but he made no comment. He was holding on to the armrest with one hand and the edge of the seat with the other, as if he were expecting the absolute worst when it came to her driving.

She checked the speedometer. She wasn't going that much above the speed limit, in spite of the fact that other cars were passing them as if they were backing up. She was a good driver, and she'd done nothing—so far—to alarm him. It occurred to her that this might be the only vehicle he could actually remember being in since the helicopter had crashed. Or he was in pain. Or both. In which case, he was doing very well.

"So what kind of music do you like?" she asked mildly.

"I like—"

"Wait, I know. You like that alternative, bastard child of bubblegum music and grunge stuff, right?"

"Yeah," he said. "Don't you?"

"Oh, please. You can't dance to it."

"You're big on dancing, are you?"

"Like you don't know," she said, and the look he gave her made her think for a moment that maybe he didn't.

"So find something," she said after a moment, gesturing to the radio.

"Scared to," he said, and when she looked at him, he actually smiled.

Almost.

"Well, if you don't want me watching the road—"

He caught her hand briefly when she reached to turn the radio on. His fingers were warm and strong around hers.

"At ease, Warren. I'll do it. You drive—or whatever you want to call this."

She acknowledged the barb with a raised eyebrow. "You want to drive?"

"Yes," he assured her.

"No way. You just stick with what you do best."

"Which is?"

"Throwing things and algebra. And swearing."

He smiled slightly and didn't say anything else. He tuned in the FM "oldie-goldie" station on the radio instead, a good choice in her opinion, and they rode for a time in silence. He began to relax a little, she thought. Or at least he let go of the arm rest, and she noticed a covert glance at her legs from time to time.

"Where are we going?" he asked when she took the Highway 27 exit.

"You'll see."

"I'd like to know ahead of time."

"Why? You don't give a damn one way or the other."

"Well, you've got me there."

"Take it easy, will you? You need a change of scenery and if you're not careful you're going to miss it. It's a beautiful day. Look at the cows and mailboxes. Try to enjoy it."

He didn't look particularly reassured, but he sighed and leaned back. She supposed he was making some kind of effort.

"So where were you yesterday?" he asked.

"When?"

"When you ditched your tutoring session. Again."

"I didn't ditch it—"

"Oh, maybe I blinked and missed seeing you?"

"I asked one of the nurses to tell you I couldn't make it."

He gave her a look. He didn't believe her for an instant.

"I *did,*" she insisted. "I guess she didn't do it. You can ask Bugs if you don't believe me."

"Oh, I believe you."

"It's the *truth.* And even if it wasn't, which it is, I passed the test, didn't I? You've got to start focusing on the big picture here, McGraw, and quit sweating the small stuff."

"Is that a fact?"

"It is."

"So, does Bugs know you're doing this?"

"This what?"

"Going wherever it is you're going—with me."

"I have no idea. There don't seem to be very

many secrets in the hospital. If he doesn't, I expect he will.''

"And that's okay with you?''

"Yes, why wouldn't it be? It's just a ride in a car, not an elopement. I don't need clearance for that.''

"I wouldn't want him to think I was…pulling rank.''

She looked at him. "I don't ask anybody for permission. I didn't even ask you if you wanted me to go browbeat your doctor. I did it all by myself, based on my assessment of the situation.''

"Which was?''

"You needed R and R, McGraw. *Bad.* Hey, there it is,'' she said, making an abrupt turn into a parking lot.

"What is this?''

"This,'' she assured him, "is barbecue lovers' heaven. Wait until you taste it.''

McGraw didn't want to go to "barbecue lovers' heaven,'' and he would have thought Rita Warren would know that. But he realized, when she pulled up three feet from the door, that she was perfectly serious. She actually expected him to get out and go in there.

"I'm really hungry,'' she said after a long period of silence on his part. "Really, *really* hungry.''

He still didn't say anything.

"You've got to do it sooner or later," she persisted.

"Do what?" he asked, daring her to say what he couldn't even bear to think about.

She took him up on the dare. "Let people see you. I told you before. You don't look that bad."

"Easy for you to say."

"No, it isn't. Some scars show. Some don't. But the effect is pretty much the same. You have to realize—"

"Rita! Don't give me any of your nickel-a-pop lectures!"

"I'm just trying to help," she said. "I owe you for the good grade."

"I don't need any help!"

"Oh, yeah. I forgot. You're not the guy so desperate to get out of the hospital a little while ago he'd even let *me* drive the getaway car."

"This isn't what I had in mind."

"But this is what you need, McGraw. Look. It's a friendly place in there. Trust me. An old World War Two vet and his wife run it. His son was in Vietnam. His grandson is a Ranger. You think the way you look is going to bother him? No, it's not," she said, answering her question for him. "Or anybody else, either. All you have to do is hobble your bad self in there, eat some barbecue—the best on this planet, mind you—and then you hobble out again. Too easy, right?"

He didn't want to talk about this anymore.

"You can do it," she whispered when he was about to tell her so. "I know you can."

"No," he said. "I can't."

He glanced at her, then back again. Her eyes held his—she had really...beautiful eyes. And legs. And probably other things.

And this was a hell of a time for him to think about any of that.

"Okay," she said. "I'll...just go in and get something and we can eat in the car." She opened the car door.

"I don't have any money," he said abruptly.

"I'm buying," she countered immediately.

"If it's bad, I'm not staying," he said.

"No, this is really great barbecue," she said, apparently deliberately misunderstanding what he meant.

"Hand me the damn crutches."

She smiled, fished them from the back seat, and got out of the car.

"Just remember to be your usual charming self," she said as she opened the door on his side. "No throwing anything."

"Yeah, yeah," he said, struggling to get to his feet. It hurt. A lot. She stood waiting patiently until he could make some attempt to walk. Another car pulled in, a family of four. They barely looked at him, even the two small children.

But when they reached the entrance, the little boy held open the door for him.

"Thanks, kid," McGraw said, hobbling through.

"You're welcome," the little boy said. "I'm a Cub Scout."

"Yeah? It's a good thing you came along. I needed a good door-holding Cub Scout right about now."

The place was moderately crowded. A few people stared. Nobody ran screaming from the building. The barbecue smelled wonderful. If it tasted half as good as it smelled, this was going to be an altogether outstanding experience.

Rita thoughtfully picked a table in a far corner instead of a booth, a place where he could stretch out his legs, well out of the main traffic area. On his way there, he caught sight of himself in a mirror hanging on the wall and immediately looked away. After all this time, his reflection still surprised him.

"Rita!" a chubby little woman called from behind the counter. "Look who's here, Tino! It's Rita!"

"Hey, darlin'!" an old man in the kitchen yelled through the order window.

"Hey, Tino," Rita called. "How's the barbecue today?"

"Best in the world," the old man called.

"It better be," Rita said. "I've been bragging on you."

"You want your usual?"

"That would be great! You want my usual, too?" she asked McGraw.

"Why not?" he said.

"Make it two, Tino!"

McGraw managed to sit without Rita's help, but she was very good at standing at the ready in case he couldn't do it—and without seeming to do so.

"I take it you've been here before," he said.

"A time or two," she said, smiling.

"Is he the World War Two vet?"

"Yeah. The Battle of the Bulge and all that fun stuff."

McGraw looked around the walls. They were covered with old tin advertisements—the Lone Ranger and his bread were very well represented and a number of soft drinks he'd never heard of. There was an old jukebox nearby. He wondered idly if it still worked.

"I guess this isn't what you're used to," she said after a moment.

"Meaning what?"

"Meaning you are—even as I speak—slumming."

"Slumming is something you do on purpose. We both know that's not how I got here."

"Oh, yeah. I forgot." She was smiling a mischievous little smile that was really getting to him.

"You are a pain in the butt, you know that?"

"Takes one to know one, McGraw."

The chubby little woman brought two large plastic cups full of tea with lemon and crushed ice. Mac sipped his immediately, thinking he'd really rather have a cold beer, but it was…good. Really good.

"Rita, honey, how long have you been back?" the woman asked.

"Oh—about a month, I guess."

"You seen Olivia?"

"Yesterday."

"I bet she's a big girl now."

"She's grown a lot, Earlene. Maybe I have, too."

"Bless your heart," Earlene said. "I am so glad to see you home again. This is where you belong."

"Well, I don't know about that. Earlene, this is Lieutenant McGraw. He's got a first name, but I don't know what it is."

"Hey, honey," she said to McGraw, and if she noted that he wasn't exactly in A-number-one shape, it didn't show. "I hope you're good and hungry. If you don't eat everything Tino sends out here, it's going to really hurt his feelings."

"I'll do my best," he said.

"So what is it?" Rita asked when the woman had gone.

"What is what?"

"Your first name."

"Everybody calls me Mac."

"I won't," she assured him.

"Why not?"

"Because I don't like it."

"Look—" he said with every bit of the irritation that remark had precipitated. He had no idea what her problem was here. He had done what she wanted. He was teaching her algebra. He had come in here like a lamb being led to the slaughter—when he sure as hell didn't want to—and she was *still* taking potshots at him.

He took a deep breath before he said something he'd regret. It was a long walk back to the hospital, especially for somebody on crutches. "I thought we were going to try to get along while we were in here."

"I'm not throwing anything," she said.

"That's a matter of opinion—"

Earlene was back with the food—two huge platters of chopped, barbecued meat, slaw, French fries, and hush puppies.

"Well?" Rita said expectantly when he took a bite and then another.

He glanced from her to Earlene.

"It's...great," he said.

Earlene went away happy, and he and Rita ate for a time in silence.

"This really is good," he said.

"Of course, it is. I don't lie. Unless I have to."

"So, do you 'omit'?" he asked, coming dangerously close to alluding to the possibility that she knew he was on the verge of being dumped. His mind darted away from the mental image of Joanna and...whoever.

"Only if I have to," she reiterated.

"Who is Olivia?"

She didn't answer him. He was about to ask again when the old man walked up.

"So, how do you like it, son?" he asked McGraw.

"It's good—the best in the world, just like you said."

Tino laughed. "What about you?" he said to Rita. "You think you don't have to say nothing?"

"No," Rita assured him. "I'm just waiting for my turn."

"Well, go ahead. I'm listening."

"It is truly wonderful. *This* is what I missed while I was gone."

"Well, now you're back. You don't have to miss it no more," he said, smiling. The smile faded. "I was real sorry to hear about your grandma's house."

"Her house? What about it?" Rita asked.

"It's burned down, honey. I thought you knew."

"No. I didn't know."

"Well, it's a sad thing—but a good thing, too, because nobody lived there. Nobody was hurt—"

"Tino!" Earlene yelled.

"What!" he yelled back. "I got to get to work before she starts chasing me with a broom. You come back again—both of you. Bring plenty of hungry friends with you."

McGraw kept glancing at Rita. The change in her was profound. She wasn't saying anything, and she wasn't eating.

"Are you okay?" he asked finally.

"Sure. Why?" she asked, going back to the mound of food on her plate. She took a few token bites and then gave up.

"You didn't know about the house burning down?"

In spite of all he could do, his question had an edge of incredulity, and he hoped she didn't notice.

"It doesn't matter," she said.

She smiled suddenly, back to her old self again, and the jukebox did work. Somebody put in some change, and the place filled with the sound of Elvis Presley. Much to the delight of the customers, Tino grabbed Earlene in passing and twirled her around and then flung her backward into a dip. Fortunately for her and anyone else in the immediate vicinity, she wasn't carrying any cups of ice tea at the time.

Rita laughed and applauded, and only when her gaze met McGraw's did the smile fade away. They finished their meal—or rather, he did. He realized on his way out to the car that this had, indeed, been what he needed—not because he had to get over the hurdle of going out in public and letting people stare at him, but because he needed to take his mind off Joanna.

God, Joanna.

At some point he was going to have to say, "Who's the guy?"

He was going to have to look at his hurt pride and his hurt feelings, and then he was going to have to look at the somewhat surprising sense of relief he felt at finally knowing what the problem between him and Joanna was.

But today he didn't want to have to deal with it. All in all, he'd much rather be hanging out—in a barbecue joint or anywhere else—with Rita Warren. It occurred to him that he wasn't thinking of her as ''Doyle's blonde'' anymore, and he didn't want to look at the reason for that, either.

When he got into the car, once again she was ready to help him if he needed it, but he managed to get situated by himself and at considerable cost. All the painful places that had essentially settled to a dull ache while he was inside and still, had been bent and stretched and jarred to the forefront by the struggle. He tried not to show how much his legs hurt, but it was all he could do to sit still.

Rita was quiet again, and when she pulled out onto the highway, she took the opposite direction from the way they had come. She cranked the radio up louder—to keep from talking, he thought—not that he felt any need for conversation. He was far too intent on trying to get a handle on the pain.

They hadn't been on the road long when she abruptly pulled off onto the narrow shoulder, jarring him hard.

''Sorry,'' she said. ''I need to do something.''

She made a three-point turn and headed back toward the barbecue place, and clearly this change in course wasn't up for discussion. He kept glancing at her, trying to read her expression.

A mile or so down the road, she made a left turn into a narrow dirt track. It was hardly more than a path, really, with weeds growing in the middle of it. It wound through a stand of pines, which suddenly gave way to open fields and finally to a small house.

Or what was left of a small house. The place had obviously burned. The stonework chimneys still stood and part of the front porch near the granite slab steps. The rest was charred rubble.

Rita pulled the car into the shade of several tall pines in the front yard and parked.

"I'll be right back," she said, getting out. She didn't give him time to protest or ask anything. She stood for a moment, staring at the burned-out shell, then walked around the side of the house and disappeared.

He rolled down the car window and waited. He listened to the birds singing, and the bees buzzing, and the sighing wind in the pines. He tried not to hurt so bad. He tried not to think about anything.

And he waited.

After a time he opened the car door to let in some of the breeze. He couldn't see Rita anywhere, couldn't hear her. The longer she was gone, the more a tiny knot of worry began to unfold in a corner of his mind. Where the hell could she be? Maybe she'd fallen or something. Maybe the place had a basement and she...

He swore. He wasn't going to sit here and wonder. He struggled to get his crutches, and he pushed the car door open as wide as it would go, knowing full well that by the time he managed to get out and on his feet, she'd arrive with some reason for her absence, which would make sense only to her and which would tick him off royally.

Again.

The ground was soft and sandy, and walking was no easy matter. He thought about calling out for her, then thought better of it. He hobbled across the yard and around the side of the house. He saw her immediately. She was sitting on the now unattached granite back steps, her head in her arms, and she was crying. Hard. He could hear that plainly as he came closer—when it was too late to turn back without her seeing him.

And she did see him. Her head came up sharply, and she began wiping furiously at her eyes, as if she thought that if she got the tears mopped up fast enough, he wouldn't notice them.

There was nothing for him to do but keep going. With considerable difficulty, he sat beside her on the steps. She kept looking at him in that way she had, the same way she'd looked at him when he'd thrown that magazine at her.

"What can I say?" he said after a moment. "I worry."

She gave a strained smile and shook her head. "You better not sit here."

"Why?"

"Because I'm not through—" she swallowed heavily "—crying."

"That's okay. Maybe you need a little…company."

"Maybe you can't get up by yourself, and you'd rather die than have me know it," she countered, the tears welling in her eyes again.

"Maybe," he said. "But I'll make the effort to get out of here, if you want."

She looked at him for a moment, but she didn't say anything else, and neither did he. She sat there beside him, the tears still rolling down her cheeks.

It had rained recently. Mac could smell the pungent odor of the wet ashes of what was left of the house. A mockingbird somewhere nearby abruptly began a loud trill, its extensive repertoire spilling over the abandoned quiet of the place. The steps were in dappled shade, but it was still warm sitting there. Every now and then, he could hear the wind high in the tops of the pines.

He stared at her profile, the line of her neck, the swell of her breasts. She really was an attractive woman, in spite of the fact that she was essentially bawling her head off. He was close enough to touch her, but he didn't. He had no idea what he should do—if anything. He had learned in the military—and from his mother—that tears in a woman were not always what they seemed. He'd seen his mother cry when she was being manipulative. He'd seen women recruits cry when they were so angry and outraged that they were just a hair away from taking some male soldier's head off. It was his opinion that a mistake men made all too often was to think that a woman's tears were a sign of weakness. At this moment, Rita Warren seemed anything but weak. She just seemed incredibly and relentlessly...sad, and he did know something about that.

"I used to live here," she said after what seemed a long time, her voice soft and husky. "Until I was eight. It was the only time I was..."

"What?" he asked when she didn't go on.

"You don't want to hear this."

"I wouldn't ask if I didn't. You were what?"

"Happy. The only time I was happy was when I lived with my grandmother—here." She took a quiet breath. "No frills, no money. And it was the best time in my whole life."

"Where were your parents?"

"Well, let's just say they weren't parenting. Some people should never have kids, you know? They were only too happy to have my grandmother take over. The difference between living with her and living with them was like the difference between heaven and hell. But...she had a stroke. An ambulance took her off to the hospital one night and I never saw her again. Some people—when they aren't a part of your life anymore—they leave a really big hole, you know?"

He did know, but he didn't say so.

"So what happened to you then?"

"I went back to dear old mom and dad. Or dear old mom and the boyfriend of the week. My dad up and left a month or so after I got there. My mother blamed me—the responsibility was just too much for him. My grandmother was the only person who ever really cared about me. Anything good in me— if there *is* anything good—is her doing. She taught me about love and honor and sacrifice…things like that. You wouldn't know it to look at me, but she did. I wanted to hang on to all that stuff she believed in—live the way she said a person ought to live. But I didn't. I miss her so much. It always helped knowing this place—this house—was still here." She sighed. "I'm glad she never knew."

"Knew what?"

She smiled instead of answering his question. "I haven't cried like this in I don't know when. Sorry—"

"You don't have to apologize to me."

"Right," she said. "I don't. I don't apologize and I don't ask for permission."

"You know, you'd have a hell of a time in the army," he said, and she laughed.

"So what about you?" she asked. "I've whined, now it's your turn."

"I don't have anything to whine about," he said, his physical condition and the crutches notwithstanding.

"I would—if I were you—what with all the backlash."

"What 'backlash'?"

"The one you get when you've been totally brainwashed—like you have."

"What are you talking about?"

"You've been conditioned by the experts, McGraw. You've been taught that the group—*your* group—is everything, right? You learned to depend on each other totally. And you stick together no matter what. Even if one—or most—of you end up dead on a mission, you still stick together—even if you die, too—"

"You are really off base here," he said.

She paid no attention. "So, when all but two of that group dies—the two left, like you and Bugs—what do you do with yourselves, McGraw? You don't know, right? Because they didn't exactly cover that in the training manual, did they? Or if they did, it's all pretty meaningless, because you can't undo that all-for-one-and-one-for-all mindset just like that, even if you wanted to. That bottom line is still there. You lived, they died. *You* abandoned the group—"

"That's enough!"

"Yes," she said. "It is. You're letting what happened to you—no, what *didn't* happen to you—drag you down, McGraw, and it's time to stop."

"What the hell do *you* know about it! They were good soldiers, and they're dead, damn it!"

She was looking steadily into his eyes. Hers were still red from crying. He sat there, trying to deny the truth of what she said, and he couldn't. Even so, he still wanted to lash out at her. He had to struggle hard to hang on to his anger. Anger was the only emotion he could trust anymore.

She abruptly smiled and briefly, even playfully, leaned against him. "Take it easy, McGraw. I just wanted you to know I understand, that's all. You may not think so, but I do. I understand that kind of stuff better than any nonmilitary personnel you'll ever meet."

She got up from the steps and walked toward the car, without looking back. He could still feel the warmth of her body against his arm. It was all he could do not to call out to her.

And say what?
And say what?

He didn't want to *say* anything. That was the problem. He wanted to *feel.* Something besides pain and guilt. He was in the process of losing everything—career, fiancée, himself—and he didn't know what to do about any of it. All he knew was that he needed—wanted—her to help him forget his misery, just for a little while. He wanted to forget, damn it. He didn't want opinions about, or explanations for, his behavior, and by God, he didn't want to be *understood.*

He stared after her, and even in his anger he couldn't keep from taking in the way she walked, the soft sway of her hips, the sunlight on her hair.

He managed to get to his feet, and he made his

way slowly back to the car. She leaned against the door on the passenger side, waiting. She didn't say anything, not then or on the drive back. They arrived at the hospital well before his curfew.

"Wait," he said when she pulled up to the door to let him out. "I'll get your money."

"My—I don't want any money."

"I don't like owing people."

"We can just call it even. I owe you for the tutoring."

"It's not the same thing. I'll get the money and have somebody bring it down to you."

Rita looked at him a long moment. "Fine," she said, but she didn't wait. When he hobbled out of his room to look for someone to take the twenty-dollar bill he estimated would cover the cost of a barbecue plate, gasoline and her time, she was waiting in the corridor.

McGraw held the money out to her. She made no attempt to come and get it. She just left him standing there. The old warhorse walked past. She didn't say anything, but she certainly looked.

McGraw ignored her. "Take the money," he said.

"You never did say anything about the test," Rita said, still avoiding his outstretched hand.

"What test?"

"The test I passed, McGraw. The algebra test. You're the reason I could do it. If it hadn't been for your tutoring—"

"Forget it. Actually, it was a real hoot for me—

for a while. Passing a high school test—'' He shrugged. ''It's not like it's a big deal.''

She stood there. He had meant to hurt her, and he hated himself for doing it. He wasn't prepared for the wounded look in her eyes, and there was no way he could take the words back.

''It was a big deal to me,'' she said. She stepped forward and snatched the money out of his hand. ''Thanks, McGraw. For everything.''

She turned and walked away, head high.

''Rita—'' he said, but she didn't hear him, or if she did, she didn't stop. As she passed one of the open doors along the corridor, she was greeted by a chorus of appreciative whistles and shouts from the patients inside. She blew her admirers a kiss and disappeared around the corner.

''You are one mean son of a bitch.''

He looked around. The old warhorse stood nearby—obviously eavesdropping.

''You really hurt her feelings, you know that,'' she continued.

''Listen! You can butt out right now—''

''Hey, your personal relationships are of no interest to me whatsoever. But you owe that girl a lot—''

''Yeah, right. I offer to help her out, and half the time she never shows up.''

''Well, your mother had something to do with one of those no-shows.''

''My— What are you talking about?''

"Mrs. McGraw heard about the magazine-throwing incident. She asked the powers-that-be to bar Rita Warren from the floor. I thought Rita should know, so I told her. I guess she decided to take my advice and stay away the weekend Mrs. McGraw was supposed to come visit."

"Your advice?"

"We have enough aggravation around here without going looking for it, Lieutenant. I think Rita is a pretty straightforward kind of person. What you see is what you get. Maybe she didn't want to tell you your mother was on her case. Maybe she didn't want to have to lie about it when you asked her why she couldn't come."

"It didn't keep her from getting here when it was convenient."

"Yeah, well, maybe she decided later your mother could go to hell. The truth is, Lieutenant—whether you or Mrs. McGraw realize it—you started to improve the very day Rita Warren began to annoy you. She was exactly what you needed. Our kind concern and empathy wasn't working—because nobody could feel as sorry for poor Lieutenant McGraw as *he* could. I told you. You *owe* her—and more than twenty bucks."

Chapter Seven

"Mama?"

"Yes, Olivia."

"Hold this."

"Hold this, please," Rita said.

"Hold this, pease," Olivia echoed.

Rita cupped her hands to take the pieces of sidewalk chalk Olivia was meticulously giving her.

"Can I draw?" Rita asked.

"No, Mama," Olivia said. "You can hold."

"Don't the holders get to draw?"

"Holders draw *next*," Olivia assured her.

Rita smiled. The two of them had been at this a long time. Olivia was in the process of covering a long section of the Beltran front sidewalk with various pastel scribbles she had dubbed "Flowers for Daddy."

And Rita was only too happy to participate. After her outing with McGraw, she had been desperate to see Olivia. Olivia was the only family she had left that really mattered to her, and seeing that burned-out house had really brought that fact home. She had needed this unscheduled visit badly, and Corey had let her come, even if it wasn't officially time for it. If she wasn't careful, she was going to end up feeling far more obligated to Corey Beltran than she ever intended feeling.

"Come on, Mama," Olivia said, moving farther down. She held both little hands out and shook them in the air to indicate how important this project was. She couldn't afford to have the help's attention wander.

"Oh, sorry," Rita said, moving closer and offering the chalk.

"Thank you, Mama."

"You're welcome, Olivia."

"See? More pretty flowers!"

"They're really nice. Daddy will like this."

"Daddy will like this," Olivia repeated, intent on filling the next section of the sidewalk.

But Rita's thoughts wandered back to the burned-out house. She hadn't meant to cry like that in front of McGraw. She rarely cried, and when she did, she never wanted an audience. Of course, she had tried to get away from him when she realized that tears were going to be inevitable. The last thing she had expected was that he would actually hobble after her. The next-to-last thing was how much she would want to talk to him about it, when she had never really spoken of her sorry childhood to anyone. Even Matt had only gotten the severely edited version. He knew she came from an incredibly indifferent family, but he'd never known that in that family there was one shining jewel. Sadie Warren, Rita's paternal grandmother. Sadie would have loved Olivia. Sadie would have even liked McGraw.

And now there was nothing of Sadie Warren left except that pile of rubble. Even her prized teacup was gone. Sadie had won it from an expensive jewelry store in Greensboro after she'd filled out a handful of tickets she'd picked up at the grand opening. The store was expensive, not the cup, but Sadie was no less thrilled with it. Actually winning something from a place where she would never have been able to shop was the main thing. The cup was plain white and really not much to look at. But when it was held up to the light, a cameo of a beautiful lady appeared in the bottom. Rita had loved that cup when she was a little girl, and she had treasured it as long as it was in her possession. She wondered idly what the landlord had done with it, with her entire collection of fancy cups and saucers, all of which had come to symbolize the time when she was happy and innocent. He probably sold the expensive ones, the gold-rimmed ones, and probably used the plain white one for an ashtray. And he probably never knew about the cameo.

She gave a quiet sigh, thinking of McGraw again. She thought that he would understand about the teacups, about what they had meant to her and why she had collected them. Even as gruff and hurtful as he had been, she still felt that he would understand anything she told him.

Anything.

She knew exactly what was happening here. It was as if she hadn't learned a thing from that broken heart she'd gotten after her completely one-sided involvement with Matt Beltran. She knew perfectly well that a woman could expect nothing but trouble and heartache if she let herself get all concerned about an indifferent man, particularly an indifferent, engaged one. The crazy thing was that she hadn't even liked McGraw at first, and here she was now, worrying about what he was doing and how he was feeling.

And whether or not he'd patched up his relationship with Joanna.

"Mama!" Olivia said, bringing her sharply back to the matter at hand. "More!"

"Oh, gosh," Rita said, handing over another piece of chalk.

Corey came onto the porch. "Time for the nap," she said, and Olivia immediately went running to her.

It surprised Rita that Olivia didn't object—but

then, she lived her life according to a comfortable routine now. Things happened the way they were supposed to happen, when they were supposed to happen—unlike when she had lived with her mother.

"Tell Mama bye," Corey said.

"Bye-bye, Mama," Olivia said dutifully. "Be a good girl."

Rita couldn't help but laugh. "Did you tell her to say that?" she asked Corey.

"No—but it's probably a good idea for all three of us."

"Thanks for letting me come. I…"

Rita didn't go on.

"It's okay," Corey said, and she didn't add "this time," but Rita could sense the unspoken phrase hanging in the air.

They both stood there. Rita wanted desperately to go hug Olivia and kiss her goodbye, but she didn't. She was afraid to. They had spent a good couple of hours together, and she didn't want to push her luck.

"Kiss her goodbye for me, will you, Corey?" she said.

"From Mama," Corey said, giving Olivia a noisy peck on the cheek and making her giggle.

"So how's the exercise class thing coming?" Corey asked as Rita turned to go.

"I've got to go look at some places for rent when I leave here."

"And school?"

"Did I tell you about school?"

"Somebody did—Lou Kurian, maybe."

Rita looked at her. Of course. Lou would keep Corey informed of how their "problem" was doing.

"It's going…pretty good," Rita said, deciding not to be offended. She shrugged.

"That's great, Rita. Well…good luck with your classes—and with the real estate."

"Yeah. Thanks."

Rita would need all the luck she could get. She had to find a place and soon. She needed a source of income and she needed to direct her energy away from worrying about Olivia and especially away from worrying about McGraw. She had told Corey the truth. Her classes at the community college weren't all that difficult—except for the algebra, of course—certainly not difficult enough to keep her mind very occupied. It was amazing to her how much she had learned in high school without realizing it. Amazing and sad. She wasn't as dumb as she had thought, and if she'd just hung in there, maybe.…

Water under the bridge, Rita! she thought abruptly. There was no point in dwelling on the past. Given a second chance and the same set of circumstances, she would make the same choices again. She knew that much about herself.

On the way to meet the real estate agent, she decided that the most sensible thing was for her not to go back to the hospital—period. No more visits with

Bugs. No more being tutored—not that she had a
choice about the tutoring. McGraw had put an end
to that and none too gently. She'd just have to visit
Bugs by phone. If she didn't see McGraw, she
couldn't possibly get involved in something that
would only lead to misery on her part. It was all
very simple—the concept if not the execution.

Rita had to force herself to concentrate on listening to the real estate agent's numerous sales pitches,
and she had all but given up on finding anything
even remotely suitable. But the very last place on
the list turned out to be more than promising. She
wondered if there were some kind of method to his
madness, if he had planned to show her the mostly
terrible rentals first—so that she'd be really thrilled
with this one.

And she *was* thrilled, so thrilled that it was hard
not to show it. The place had once been some kind
of store in a strip mall on the boulevard. The maroon
industrial carpeting was still down. It needed a good
shampooing, of course, and she'd have to paint the
walls some other color besides the current weak-hot-
chocolate beige. And she'd have to figure out some
way to obscure the huge plate-glass windows—no
woman in her right mind would want to come to an
exercise class where there was such a huge potential
for an audience. But it was spacious enough for her
needs, and parking wouldn't be a problem. Now if
she could just afford it.

She made an offer to the real estate agent—less

than the rent the owner was asking, with the understanding that she would make a few improvements and she would also be eliminating a blight to his property by occupying an empty storefront. Then she sat back to wait—and she was back to trying not to think about McGraw.

The red light was blinking on her answering machine when she got home. It was McGraw, absolutely the last person she expected to hear from.

"Rita, it's—you didn't—" he said in a rush, as if he were in a big hurry to get it out before he changed his mind.

There was a commotion in the background—people talking—a woman talking.

"Didn't what, McGraw?" Rita said impatiently.

But there was nothing else except the sound of him hanging up the phone.

She stood staring at the answering machine. On impulse, she rewound the message and punched the Play button.

"Rita—"

She stopped it immediately and rewound it again.

"Rita—"

It was the only time since the first day they met that she remembered him ever saying her name.

Where is she?

It had been over three weeks now—almost four, and if Rita had come back to the hospital, she'd managed to do it without McGraw seeing her, which wasn't likely, considering the vigil he was keeping. He wanted to ask Bugs about it, but he didn't quite have the nerve. He had to comfort himself with the fact that if Bugs was worried about anything—like Rita's whereabouts—it didn't show.

McGraw had decided on any number of occasions that he was *not* going to think about Rita Warren— without much luck. He'd tried calling, but then he bailed out before he made a complete fool of himself. What could he say, anyway?

How about I'm sorry? he thought ruefully.

Now there was an idea that was really high speed. He could apologize. He shouldn't have put her down like that. And if he was any kind of man at all, he'd bite the bullet and tell her so.

The burns on his legs were healing. He wanted to tell her that, too. And he wanted to know how the algebra class was going—and if she'd gone back to the barbecue joint or her grandmother's house. He wanted to know everything, anything she would deign to tell him.

He had talked to Joanna several times. It amazed him how normal she sounded, chatting about people they both knew and when she would be able to come see him. She went all out to keep up appearances. She'd even ended the conversations by saying she loved him.

Well, perhaps she did in some way, just not the way that would keep her from wanting another man—a whole man, one who had a job she could be proud of and who wouldn't leave her and go chasing all over the world every time she turned around. But he wasn't feeling sorry for himself in one respect, at least. He had—used to have—a career he loved. Not many people could say that. If anything, he felt sorry for Joanna. She was too honorable not to stay with him as long as he was like this and she thought he needed her—and not honorable enough to keep from having somebody on the side.

His mother kept insisting that he come home for a weekend visit. Getting leave from the hospital long enough to do that wouldn't be a problem, not with the progress he was making. The problem was the fact that he didn't want to go. He knew that he wasn't going to be able to put off a confrontation with Joanna indefinitely—he didn't really want to. It was over, as far as he was concerned, even if she didn't go riding off into the sunset with the new guy. It was just that he couldn't get himself into the good old Airborne "can do" mindset enough to want to deal with anything else unpleasant. It took all his energy just to heal.

He didn't know what he wanted—yes, he did. He wanted to see Rita Warren. In spite of everything he could do, she was all he thought about, asleep and awake. In spite of the daily ordeal of physical therapy and the skin scrubs, in spite of the phone calls from Savannah, he still found time to…miss her.

Or maybe he just missed the aggravation. And the

long legs. And that just-who-do-you-think-you-are-buster attitude. She made him laugh. She made him mad. She made him think he could be himself again.

He was so restless. When he couldn't stay put any longer, he dragged himself to the nearest exit with every intention of taking what, for him, would pass as a short walk. In spite of his improvement, getting from Point A to Point B still left a lot to be desired when it came to his form.

It was a hot afternoon, but he thought he could stand it for a little while. Unfortunately he forgot how much physical effort it would take just to make it to the first available shade. He decided to abandon the plan when he was only a few yards from the door. On his way back inside he ran into Bugs, who was being pushed along by one of the medical staff and obviously en route to another location.

"You going somewhere, Doyle?" he asked with no thought as to the appropriateness of the question. His only thought was that Doyle might be in the process of being transferred to another hospital, one closer to his family—in which case, Rita absolutely wouldn't be coming by again.

"Sir, yes, Sir," Doyle said.

McGraw waited, leaning heavily on his crutches but still conveying that he expected details.

He had no opportunity to get them. A white church van pulled up—one with a lift to accommodate wheelchairs. The civilian driver, an old man with a big grin, had no compunction whatsoever about keeping McGraw from continuing his not-particularly-subtle interrogation.

"Buck's Taxi Service—right on time!" the old man said to Doyle. "You ready to go, son?"

Doyle looked at McGraw. McGraw gave him a curt nod and stood back out of the way. There was nothing left to do but struggle inside.

He was hot and sweaty and generally miserable by the time he reached his floor. The old warhorse looked up when he passed the nurses' station.

"A party," she said when he was close enough.

"What?" he asked, frowning.

"If you can't find Doyle, he's gone to a party."

He looked at her, waiting. She didn't say anything else. She absolutely was going to make him pull the information out of her.

"What party?" he asked in spite of everything he could do. In an effort to seem disinterested in spite of having just caved, he studiously read her name tag: Meehan.

"The one you would have been invited to if you'd played your cards right."

"Am I supposed to know what that means?"

"Nope."

"I guess you expect me to ask."

"Yep," she said, grinning. "Anything worth knowing is worth asking about, Lieutenant."

He sighed and shifted his weight on his crutches.

"Okay. What party are you talking about?"

"The one for Rita—Warren," she added, apparently in the event his memory was attached to his temper—and since he was in the process of losing the latter, the former might go right along with it.

He started hobbling again. The conversation was dangerously close to getting personal.

"It's at Matt Beltran's place," she continued anyway. "Sergeant Beltran—you know the one. He and his wife are throwing it. Corey Beltran makes the best chocolate cake on the face of this earth. You've missed a truly wonderful experience."

McGraw kept going.

"Don't you want to know *why* they're throwing it?" the old warhorse called after him.

He stopped. "Okay, why?" he said. This woman would never make it easy for him.

"Rita got her G.E.D."

"Already?" he asked in surprise.

"The way I understand it, somebody or other had paid the money to challenge the course—only this person got sick—appendicitis or something. So Rita—being Rita—decided to step in and take it. No use letting all the arrangements go to waste, right? So she paid the person the price of challenging the course, and the rest is history."

"She...passed," he said, more to himself than to her.

"Aced it, she said. Took her all day, but she did it."

"You talked to her?"

"When she called to see if she could get Bugs

out long enough to join the festivities. Talk about logistics. Only Rita could pull a van with a wheelchair lift out of her hat like that.''

He didn't say anything. He started walking again.

"She asked about you."

He stopped and looked at her. "Right."

"No, she *always* asks about you. Every single time she calls. Now, what does that look mean? I don't think Joanna will mind."

"She won't, but Bugs might."

"Why would he? Oh, you didn't think Bugs and Rita had a thing going, did you?"

He didn't say anything, because that was exactly what he thought.

"Don't you want to know what I tell her when she calls?"

"Not if I can help it."

"I always say you're the same old ugly pain in the butt."

He tried not to respond to that, but a smile got away from him.

"Thanks a lot, Meehan. Anything else you'd like to tell me before I move on?"

"Nope. That's about it—except for one small observation."

"*That,* I'm not going to ask about," he assured her.

"You could be partying tonight, McGraw," she said anyway, leaning over the desk to call after him. "Instead of staying here with me."

And it's a hell of a note, too, he thought as he maneuvered down the corridor. He eventually made it to the chair by his bed, and he sat for a while with no conscious plan in mind, until he suddenly reached for the phone book.

It didn't take him long to locate what he thought was Sergeant Beltran's phone number. He dialed it quickly, not giving himself time to rethink the advisability of doing so. Someone—a woman—answered on the third ring. He knew immediately that he had the right place. He could hear laughter and conversation in the background, and music, all the sounds associated with people having a good time.

"Is Rita Warren there?" he asked.

"Yes, she is."

"Could she...come to the phone?"

"Just a minute."

He didn't have to wait long. If he had, he would have bailed out like he did the last time.

But Rita was there almost immediately.

"Hello?" she said, and he closed his eyes.

"Hello..." she said again.

"Mama! Look!" a child said in the background.

"Rita, it's me," he said finally. "McGraw."

"McGraw—what? Now, this *is* a surprise. How did you know I was here?"

"The grapevine," he said.

"Oh, you mean Meehan."

Rita paused, apparently to give him a chance to say something. He didn't.

"So what can I do for you?" she asked finally.

"I need...cake," he said crazily.

"You're going to have to run that by me again, Lieutenant."

"I...heard you were celebrating the G.E.D. And I heard about Mrs. Beltran's chocolate cake. I thought maybe you'd like to bring me some." Even he thought he was being outrageous, but *no guts, no glory.*

She laughed, but she didn't turn him down. Or hang up.

"Is there any left?" he said, plunging on, because he'd started in this direction and given his lack of planning, he decided it was as good as any. "Chocolate cake, I mean."

"I don't know. Corey!" she yelled to someone in the background. "Any cake left?"

"Sure," a woman answered. "There's one that hasn't been cut."

"I've got a special request here—Lieutenant Mc-Graw—from the hospital. What do you say?"

"I'll pack him up some right now," the woman answered. "Of course, I'll have to hide it," she added, apparently because of the protests from the cake-eaters in the crowd.

"Okay," Rita said to him. "You want cake, you got cake. I'll send it back with Bugs—"

"I thought maybe you could bring it," McGraw said, still making up the plan as he went along. He wanted to see her, and he wasn't going to let her

pretend that she hadn't heard him before, when he'd
given her the opportunity to come here.

He waited for her to say something.

"This *is* the magazine-throwing McGraw," she
said after a moment.

"Affirmative."

"Okay. I'll bring the cake. But don't let me see
anything throwable when I get there."

Chapter Eight

"Am I too late to make a delivery?" Rita asked, holding up the cake as she got off the elevator.

"No," Meehan said. "McGraw can use the company—and the cake. He's around that way. Sitting at the end of the hall."

"Thanks."

"Rita," Meehan said when she turned to go. "Don't let him make you think he hasn't missed having you come for the algebra tutoring."

Nobody to pick on, Rita thought, wondering how Meehan knew the cake was for McGraw. Bugs must have told her. She had been surprised when McGraw called her out of the blue like that, especially at the Beltrans' place. Bugs, however, might never get over the shock.

The floor was quiet. She noted that most of the rooms were dark as she passed. It must be later than she thought, and McGraw must really need the company if Meehan was bending the rules like this.

Rita rounded the corner, and she could see McGraw, sitting in a wheelchair at the far end as predicted. He watched as she walked toward him down the corridor, but he didn't say anything, didn't acknowledge her in any way.

I've seen that look before, Rita thought. *If he pretends the cake delivery wasn't his idea, he's going to be wearing it.*

She stopped a few feet in front of him and waited for him to say something. The ball was in his court as far as she was concerned.

"You brought it," he said finally.

"Of course. I said I would."

"Yeah, well," he said, apparently alluding to that one time when she hadn't shown up for the tutoring. Actually, two times, but he hadn't gotten the message she'd left the second time, and the first time she'd let being on his mother's hit list and not being able to see Olivia stampede her. She'd been reliable since—or she would have been, given the opportunity.

She handed him the huge piece of tightly wrapped cake and a plastic fork. "So what's this all about?" she asked.

"What do you mean?"

"I mean, what do you want, McGraw? And don't

tell me chocolate cake. Let's just get to the bottom line.''

He looked at the cake. "This looks good. Thanks.''

"The bottom line?'' she said again.

"Why didn't you ever finish high school?'' he asked instead of answering.

She frowned, wondering where *that* had come from.

"No comment,'' she said. She sat on a nearby metal and plastic all-purpose chair, and she wondered if McGraw had it here just for that purpose.

"I'm serious,'' he persisted. "I know you're smart enough. You're a damn good student. Why didn't you finish high school when you had the chance?''

"Why are you asking me this?''

"Because I want to know more about you.''

"Why? So you can cut me off at the knees again?''

"I didn't—'' He stopped and took a quiet breath. "I wasn't— The other day, I was…aggravated— because what you'd said hit a little too close to home. And I took it out on you. I'm sorry I did that.''

She gave him a look.

"I'm sorry,'' he said again. "What? You don't believe me?''

"No,'' she said pointedly.

"Answer the question anyway.''

"I can't. You wouldn't understand."

He smiled slightly. "Because we're from two different worlds?"

"The 'different worlds' thing doesn't even begin to apply to you and me."

"Try me."

"No, thanks, McGraw. You don't know how the other half lives."

"I might surprise you."

"Oh, I doubt it. You come from a two-parent household, right? Belonged to the Boy Scouts, sang in the church choir, took tennis and piano lessons—"

"Clarinet," he interrupted. "So?"

"I repeat. You don't know how the other half lives."

"Then explain it to me."

"No, thanks."

Looking into his eyes, it occurred to her that she'd had very much this same conversation with Bugs—about McGraw. Bugs hadn't thought she could understand their military mindset, but, in McGraw's case, she had. It also occurred to her how much she wanted to tell him…whatever he wanted to know, how much she wanted to go back to that brief rapport they'd shared at Sadie's burned-out house.

She kept looking at him. The injuries on his face were better, so much so that he no longer avoided her eyes the way he once had.

But she was still puzzled about his reason for asking her to come here.

"You told me about your grandmother," he said.

"Only because I was coming unglued."

"Yeah, well, we all do that sometimes."

"Some of us more than others," she said, and this time he did smile.

But he didn't say anything. He only nodded, his very subtle acknowledgment that she was holding her own and he appreciated her skill.

"Congratulations on getting your G.E.D.," he said after a moment.

"Thank you."

"You're going on with the algebra?"

"If it kills me," she said.

"The party was...nice, I guess."

"Yes."

"Did you know about it ahead of time or was it a surprise?"

"Why?"

"I was wondering why I wasn't invited."

She laughed. "Oh, sure. Your sunny self is the first person who'd come to mind if I wanted to staff a party."

"So, was it a surprise or not?"

"You wouldn't believe what a surprise it was," she said.

"Lot of people there?"

"A few."

"Legs or—"

"Mostly legs," she said, using the Airborne term for people who *don't* jump out of airplanes for a living.

What is this? she thought.

They sat for a time in silence. He was still holding the cake.

"Don't you want to eat that?" she asked.

"Later," he said. "Right now I…"

He didn't finish whatever he was going to say, and she didn't press him. She watched him closely, trying to read his mood. He was different in more ways than just his looks.

"I miss the—" he said abruptly, but he didn't finish that thought, either.

"Well, you would, wouldn't you?" she said.

"You don't know what I was going to say."

"Sure I do. You miss the Airborne thing. Running around in the woods. Jumping out of C-130's. Never knowing when you're going to be on the first transport out of here and heading to the other side of the world. A thrill a minute, am I right? And all of a sudden it's gone."

She clearly was right, but he wasn't about to say so.

"See?" she said. "I told you I understood more than any nonmilitary person you'd ever meet."

"And how do you account for that?"

"I've hung out with a lot of paratroopers," she said truthfully. "I *understand.*"

"That's what I want to do," he said.

"Hang out with paratroopers?" she asked, smiling.

"No. Understand. I want to understand you."

"Not in this lifetime, McGraw."

"No, see, I usually know what's going on with people. Bugs and the rest of them—I never had any problem reading them. But I can't read you. I think something really drives you—but I don't know what the hell it is."

"Well, we're not going there. It's a big waste of time."

This conversation was way too far from any "bottom line" she might have anticipated, and his remark about something driving her only served to point out how different they really were. He couldn't know about something like that. He'd never been on the outside looking in. He'd never done anything so stupid and so bad as she had. He'd never had a "past" to live down, and her past was bad enough to make that mother of his do double back flips.

She moved to get up. She had every intention of leaving.

"Wait. I wanted to ask you a favor," he said quickly. He reached out to keep her, then seemed to think better of it.

"*Another* one?"

"Yeah. It's...kind of a big one. I don't want to ask anybody else."

"What is it?"

"I have to go home."

"Have to?"

"Yeah. I don't want to go, but the family is kind of pushing for it. And there are some things I need to take care of."

She looked at him, thinking he might elaborate as to what those "things" might be. He didn't, of course.

"And home is?" she asked.

"Savannah."

"So you want me to water your plants? Walk your dog?" she asked, unable to resist being flippant because he was being so serious.

"No. I want you to go with me."

Rita was sitting at the back steps when Matt came out. Tough military guy or not, she startled him.

"Rita! What the hell!"

"You need to do something about that language," she said mildly. "I don't want Olivia learning those words."

He exhaled sharply. "What are you doing here?"

"I'm waiting for your wife and son to get back from taking Olivia to play school."

"Why?"

"I want to talk to her."

"About what?" he asked, and she did *not* like his demanding tone.

"None of your business, Sergeant. She knows I'm here and it's got nothing to do with you. It's a...girl thing. Corey is the only person I know who can maybe give me some insight.''

''Insight?''

''Yes, insight! If anybody knows about mules and thoroughbreds in the same harness, she does.''

''Rita, what are you talking about?''

''Oh, go make the world safe for democracy, will you? Your presence really isn't required here.''

''Rita—''

''What!''

''Nothing. Have a good day,'' he said, and marched off to his car.

She didn't have to wait long. Corey arrived, and being Corey, she arrived with bagels, hot coffee and orange juice in one hand—and her son in the other.

''Let's eat out here,'' Corey said, leading the way around to the side porch and a wrought-iron table and chairs. She set the bags she was carrying down on the table and offered Rita the baby boy, who rested happily on her hip.

''Come here, handsome,'' Rita said, holding out her hands. Once again she was struck by how happy this child was—and by Corey's trust in her. It was easy to see why Matt loved Corey so much.

Corey returned after a moment with napkins, a couple of blue-and-white plates, two matching coffee mugs and a no-spill baby cup. She poured some of the juice into the baby cup and handed it to Rita.

''Does Olivia like play school?'' Rita asked as she helped the baby drink. The juice more than met his expectations, and he bounced up and down for another sip.

"Yes, but it took her a while."

"Why?"

Corey didn't answer her.

"Oh," Rita said. She didn't have to be a rocket scientist to figure out that whenever Olivia found herself in a strange new situation, just maybe she would think she was being left behind again.

What am I doing? Rita thought. *I can't talk to Matt's wife about this.*

"What's wrong?" Corey asked after a moment.

"Nothing," Rita said automatically.

"Right," Corey acknowledged. "Silly me." She plunked a bagel on a plate and pushed it in Rita's direction.

Rita accepted it, but she didn't really want it. It was just another friendly gesture on Corey's part. Rita had no idea how anybody could be like her— kind all the time, as if she didn't even have to think about it. It was like hanging out with Melanie in *Gone With the Wind.*

Rita looked around her, shifting the baby's position in her lap. It was just that it was so *nice* here. Shade, and flowers, and birds singing.

And the wind in the pines.

Corey didn't press her for any more information. Rita handed the baby over, and they ate for a time in silence.

"Okay, something's wrong," Rita admitted

abruptly. "But I don't want advice. I'm no good at taking advice and never have been. All I want is for you to listen to the situation and then tell me what you think. And you might as well know it's killing me to even bring this up—to you of all people. I don't have anybody else to talk to, so I want you to keep that in mind."

"Okay," Corey said. "Go ahead."

But Rita just sat there. This was a lot harder than she expected.

"Does it have something to do with Lieutenant McGraw?" Corey asked.

"What makes you think that?" Rita said, immediately on the defensive.

"The look on your face when he called last night. And…the look on Bugs's face."

Rita sighed. "Okay, it's McGraw. But he's just a friend. That's all. I like him and I—he's engaged, for God's sake—but I don't know if he saw Joanna planting a big fat wet one on the jerk in the car or not—and I don't know why he wants me along when he goes home—when it's his first visit since he was hurt so bad and his mother hates me already—"

"Hold it!" Corey said. "I know who McGraw is. I know he and Bugs are the only ones who survived that helicopter crash. I know he's been hard to handle—he insisted on coming back to the hospital here, but he doesn't want to do anything the doctors tell him. But that's all I know. So could we start from there?''

"I'll try."

"Please do."

Rita launched into what she hoped was a coherent account of the McGraw situation, from her first meeting with him to this request of his to go with him when he went home to Savannah tomorrow.

"Well," Corey said after a moment. "Did he tell you why he wanted you to go along?''

"He *said* he couldn't stand the thought of having all these people coming by to see how bad he was *really* hurt and then falling all over themselves trying not to say the wrong thing. He wants me to drive him down there so he can just leave whenever he's had enough. He said if somebody in the family comes up here and gets him, then he's stuck.''

"That makes sense, doesn't it?''

"Oh, yeah—if you forget all about Joanna and his mother.''

"You've lost me again.''

"His mother tried to have me barred from the floor he's on—because I threw that magazine back at him, and she heard about it and had a fit. But they don't get along—Bugs told me that—''

"McGraw and his mother.''

"Right. She doesn't like him being in the army in the first place—it's not good enough for her—and she's always trying to take over and he's always digging in. And then Joanna… If he saw her kissing that guy in the parking lot—well, what better way to stick it to her *and* his mother than to show up with me?''

''You think that's what he's doing?''

''Yes. No. Oh, I don't know!''

''Well, why don't you just ask him?''

''Because I don't know if he knows his mother tried to keep me out of the hospital. If he doesn't, I wouldn't want to tell him. I mean, you can't go around whining about somebody's mother right to his face, can you?''

''Not if you care about him,'' Corey said, but Rita let that slide.

''And I don't know if he knows about Joanna and that guy she's got on the side. I *think* he saw them, but I don't know for sure. If he doesn't, I *really* don't want to be the one to tell him about that.''

''You're sure about the other guy?''

''I saw the clench. It wasn't what you'd call just friends.''

''So what do you want to do? Do you want to drive him home or not?''

''I...wouldn't mind doing it. I owe him for the tutoring, see. It's like he trusts me to do it. To get him in there—and get him out if he needs to leave, you know?''

''Then why don't you do it? He might be hoping to rattle some cages, but really, what if he is?''

''What if he is? Corey, are you serious?''

''If he saw the kiss, then his pride has to be hurt.

It's not as if you don't know what's what here. Maybe his fiancée needs a little dose of reality and you can help him out with that, too. If the main thing is what you just said, Rita—he trusts you to get him out of there when he can't take it anymore—and you're friends, then what's a little icing on the cake going to hurt?''

"Well, maybe I can't take it, either. Bugs says Mrs. McGraw is a handful."

"Oh, like you're not."

"Corey!" Rita chided her. "Why don't you say what you *really* think?"

"I do—and so do you. And if you think you can't hold your own with McGraw's mother, then drop him off at the door."

"And do what for two days?"

"Sit in the car?" Corey suggested.

"I might not have a choice when his mother realizes who I am."

Both of them looked around when a car pulled into the drive. It was Lou Kurian. Just what Rita needed.

"I thought that was you, Rita," Lou said as she walked up. "I just wanted to say congratulations— sorry I missed the party last night."

"Thanks," Rita said. She refrained from mentioning that she hadn't known Lou was invited.

"So, what are you girls up to?" Lou asked.

"Nothing much," Corey said. "Pull up a chair."

"Actually we're talking about whether or not I should drive McGraw to Savannah," Rita said, deciding she'd rather Lou hear it from her firsthand than behind her back after she'd gone.

Lou looked at her. "Hospital patient Lieutenant McGraw with the fiancée?"

"That's the one," Rita said. She had to admire Lou's stellar memory.

"So, does the fiancée know you're the new chauffeur?" Lou said as she sat down.

"I don't know."

"But I expect you're going to give this driving thing a whirl so you can find out."

"Maybe."

"Maybe? Rita, how do you get yourself into these situations? That's what I want to know," Lou said testily. "You're just like a moth looking for a flame, and if there isn't one, that's okay, because you're flying around with a dang box of matches in your pocket."

"I didn't do anything!" Rita said. "All I said was, 'Do you know anything about algebra?' And I don't need anybody yelling at me. I just need to decide if I want to drive him to Savannah, that's all."

"No, you do *not* want to drive him to Savannah or anyplace else," Lou said. "Haven't you been through enough trouble and heartache without getting into another triangle—excuse me, Corey," she added, because of her heavy-handed reference to Rita's history with Matt.

"It's just a three-and-a-half hour drive, Lou. It's not what you think."

"Of course it's what I think!" Lou said.

"He needs my help—"

"Oh, God," Lou said, rolling her eyes heavenward. "Rita, you are standing right in the middle of the interstate here. Don't you see that big old truck coming? The one with Poor Hurt Lieutenant McGraw Needs Me But He's Got A Fiancée written all over it."

"You don't know the details here," Rita insisted.

"And I don't want to. Don't I have enough to think about with having to worry about you getting into some kind of fistfight with somebody's intended? And right when things are going good for you, too. You'll probably end up on the six o'clock news *and* in jail."

"There isn't going to be any fistfight with McGraw's fiancée. The fistfight will be with his mother," Rita said, trying not to smile, and Corey laughed.

"Okay, okay," Lou said. "I get it. You two think this is funny. Rita, you're going to do what you're going to do—I know that. But don't say I didn't warn you. Anybody going to eat that other bagel?"

"Take it," Corey said.

"And the orange juice?"

"It's all yours."

"Great," Lou said. "Hey, baby boy," she said abruptly. "Don't look at me like that—you're not ready for bagels, yet. You got to have lots and lots of teeth.''

The baby grinned and bounced.

''I don't know what to wear,'' Rita said to no one in particular. ''What do you think I should wear?''

''Wear *where?*'' Lou asked pointedly.

Rita ignored the remark. The more she thought about it, the more making this trip seemed the thing to do. Once and for all, it would put everything in perspective for her where McGraw was concerned. The truth was, she didn't really know how the ''other half'' lived, either. If she took him to Savannah, she could see, firsthand—assuming she was allowed to get out of the car. She wasn't nearly as thick-skinned as she liked to pretend. Her memories of Bitsy Corrin-Welch were too vivid for her not to view an encounter with Mrs. McGraw—on her own turf—with fear and trembling. She knew exactly what the woman would think. She would without a doubt think that Rita Warren was after her son, and she would respond to that threat accordingly.

''I've got some new clothes I haven't even taken the tags off,'' Rita said. ''You know, Corey, I showed you the jacket and the skirt—when I visited Olivia time before last.''

''Rita, that wasn't a skirt, that was a belt. You wear that, and there *will* be a fistfight.''

''Oh, I guess you think I can't just be myself. That wouldn't do at *all,* would it? I guess you think I ought to dress more like *you.*''

"Can't hurt," Lou said with her mouth full of bagel.

"You've got great legs," Corey said. "You've got great—everything. But I think maybe you ought to show it all off as you're leaving, not when you arrive. There's no point in striking those matches Lou was talking about."

As much as Rita would have hated to admit it, that made perfect sense. She could go in quietly— and leave with a bang—if she wanted to. Her choice.

She sat there, trying to remember what Joanna had been wearing the two times she'd seen her. No "belts," that's for sure. Nothing plunging. Joanna was tasteful. Classy.

I could do that, she thought, but she'd have to have help. She was strictly from the if-you've-got-it-flaunt-it school. She'd had to be. It would take a stronger will than hers to cover up the only talents she'd ever had.

"Okay, everybody," she said abruptly. "Let's go shopping."

It surprised her when both women took her up on the suggestion. Lou made a quick phone call to get three hours of personal leave approved to cover their trip to the mall, and away they all went. The baby fell asleep before they reached the first store on the list. After a parade of dressing rooms and much discussion, Rita finally bought two outfits, both of them very "Not Rita."

"Will you come by and let me see how you look

before you leave?'' Corey asked as she got into her car to go pick up Olivia at play school.

''No,'' Rita said.

''Please,'' Corey said. ''I've put a lot of effort into this. I want to see the final result. Olivia will, too. She loves new dresses. It doesn't matter if they're hers or not.''

Rita sighed. She supposed that she could do with someone's final approval. ''No laughing. I mean it.''

''I promise.''

''Okay, then. Tomorrow—before I go pick up McGraw—if I go pick up McGraw. If he's got any sense at all, he'll change his mind about doing this.''

But he didn't change his mind. He called her shortly after she got home to give her instructions to pick him up at the front entrance of the hospital. He would meet her there, after his dressings had been redone and the doctor gave his final okay for the trip.

Rita slept fitfully, her mind busy revising her wardrobe plans most of the night. When it didn't *matter* what she wore. She knew that. She was simply the chauffeur—who was going to get to spend the night in the big house. She'd be there from Friday evening until early Sunday morning, tops. McGraw had to be back at the hospital for another dressing change, if he didn't run out on his big homecoming sooner.

Rita arrived at the Beltran house shortly after

noon. Both Corey and Lou were waiting. Rita would have to say that *they* behaved very nicely. Matt, who happened to wander home while she was still there, was another matter.

"Holy—" he said when he saw her, and he would have added a word totally inappropriate for Olivia's budding vocabulary if Corey hadn't all but tackled him by the back door.

"No, no, *no,* Sergeant," she said, one arm around his neck and her other hand over his mouth.

"No, no, no," Olivia said, hugging his knees.

"You didn't want to say *that,* now, did you?" Corey asked him.

His shoulders were shaking with laughter.

"And now that you've had a moment to reflect, you can see the wisdom of completely revising whatever statement you were about to make, can't you?"

He dutifully nodded.

"Good," Corey said, releasing him.

Matt cleared his throat. "Well, Rita," he said. "D— Darn!"

And with that he picked up Olivia and left the room.

"That's it, I'm changing," Rita said.

"No!" Lou and Corey said in unison.

"You look really, *really* pretty," Corey said.

"Yes, you do," Lou said. "I especially like what you've done with your hair. You look so delicate, positively…ethereal."

But Rita had had very little experience in accepting compliments from other women. Or from men, either, for that matter—unless wolf whistles and barking counted.

Olivia came running in from wherever Matt had taken her. "Pretty Mama!" she said, coming straight to Rita to be picked up.

"See?" Corey said.

"You think Mama's dress is pretty?" Rita asked her, holding her close for a moment and savoring her little girl smell.

"Yes!" Olivia answered, leaning back and grinning.

"Okay," Rita decided, hugging her again. Who else's approval could she possibly need?

She said her goodbyes and left for the hospital, wondering all the way there if she was doing the right thing. She tried to keep in mind what Corey had said. If McGraw was a friend, then why not help him with this?

She didn't see him out front when she arrived. After a third pass by the hospital entrance, she found a parking space and went inside looking for him. He wasn't in his room, and neither was Bugs. She waited round for a while, then finally went to check at the desk.

"Meehan—" she said, running into the nurse on the way. "Do you know where McGraw is?"

"Yeah. He and Bugs are having some kind of

conversation in the day room—but I wouldn't interrupt.''

"Why not?''

"I just wouldn't. McGraw had a rough morning with the dressings change, and they both had that look. You know the one I mean. The No Unauthorized Personnel Beyond This Point one.''

Rita knew exactly the expression Meehan meant. She'd been on receiving end enough times—only she would have described it more as Trespassers Will Be Shot.

She stood around and waited near the doorway to his room. And waited. Occasionally she chatted with the help. He finally arrived, and his reaction when he saw her was a little more subtle than Matt Beltran's had been—but not much. She didn't comment on his double-take, or on the unabashed attention he gave her when she went to get his gear bag. She lasted all the way down on the elevator, but by the time she had thrown his one bag into the trunk of her car, she couldn't take it anymore.

"What?'' she asked pointedly.

"Nothing,'' he said innocently.

"Then what are you looking at?''

"Nothing. You just look different today, that's all.''

"Different. How different?''

"I don't know. *Different*.''

"Different in a bad way?''

"No.''

"What then?"

"Rita, what do you want me to say?"

"I don't want you to say anything, McGraw. Nothing. Not one word." She opened the car door for him, whether he wanted her to or not—and none too gently. "Just get in, will you?"

She waited until he was situated, and only then did she glance in his direction. He was grinning. She ignored it, but she made no attempt to leave.

"Can we go now, please?" he asked after a moment.

She sighed and started the car.

"You look damn good, Warren" he said as she pulled away from the curb. "And you know it."

Chapter Nine

The drive to Savannah took three hours and thirty-nine minutes. McGraw had very little to say, and as the trip progressed, Rita grew more and more thankful for a working radio. Meehan had told her that he'd had a "rough morning," and Rita wanted to attribute his lack of conversation to whatever procedure he'd had to endure and not to the private conversation he'd had with Bugs. He was clearly in pain and had been for some time, but mostly, he stared out the window. Rita took every opportunity to keep glancing at him while he was so seemingly unaware. She did care what happened to him, no matter how hard she tried not to. She cared enough to be going down this all too familiar road again—and she didn't mean the road to Savannah.

You never learn, Rita, she thought. *You absolutely never learn.*

It wasn't until they were crossing a huge suspension bridge into the city that McGraw began to take some notice that she was in the car with him.

"You should have gotten out and walked around a little bit at the rest stop," Rita said.

He made an impatient gesture. "Too late now. You're going to have to get into the left lane A.S.A.P."

"Oh, great," she said, looking at the long line of traffic exactly where she needed to be. It took some doing, and the drivers in the other lane were less than happy with her take-no-prisoners maneuver, but she managed.

"Now what?" she asked in spite of the incredulity on his face.

"Keep going for—bear to the left, bear left!" he suddenly yelled, just in time for her to do it.

"Do you always drive like this?" he asked, still holding on to the door.

"You know it would help if you could give me just a little warning. Anyway, what do you care? You're a steely-eyed military man. You can take it."

He smiled. He might not be smiling more often, but the smiles did seem to come more easily.

"Left again," he said. "Now we're going to me-ander. I want you to see the Squares."

When he said "squares," it hadn't occurred to her that he meant "parks." And they did "meander," around the edges of any number of them, McGraw giving her the names and a short history of each as they rode past. Eventually they came into what she assumed to be a residential district. Huge trees and beautiful old houses lined the streets, and there seemed to be a lot of people out walking—some in groups and some with their dogs.

"Right turn," he said as they approached an intersection. "One block, then hang another right. Then there's a narrow driveway on the left—about halfway down the block. Turn in there."

She found the drive, and "narrow" was an understatement. It was a good thing she was driving a small car. The driveway led along the backside of several three story houses to a kind of courtyard edged with garages made out of hewn granite blocks. She wondered if they'd once been carriage houses, only now the "carriages" were all expensive foreign-made cars. She didn't see anything remotely resembling a parking space, and she didn't see any way out of the cul-de-sac without backing up.

"Just stop right here. We'll worry about where to park later," he said.

She stopped the car where he said, and sat behind the wheel, saying nothing. The sun went behind a cloud. She looked up at the sky. It was going to rain soon. She gave a quiet sigh.

"What's wrong?" he asked.

"Nothing."

"Are you okay?"

"Who me? You're the one with the crutches. Mc-Graw, I..."

"What, Rita? You're not going to run out on me now, are you?"

"This is not a good idea, and you know it. I've got no business being here. How about I just let you out and—"

"I need you here."

"No, you don't. Somebody else could have done this."

"There is no one else. You're not afraid of my mother, are you?" he asked, getting directly to the bottom line.

"Yes," she said without hesitation.

"She knows you're coming with me. She's not going to be surprised."

Or happy, Rita thought.

"You told her specifically who I was—Rita Warren, the magazine-thrower."

"I didn't have to tell her."

"Oh, great. And she said what?"

"She just...had some questions."

"I'll just bet. Did she get any answers?"

McGraw looked at her. "I didn't have any answers to give her—except that you're Bugs Doyles' friend. All I have is the situation."

"Which is?"

He made no attempt to answer her.

"Here they come," he said of a distinguished-looking man and a very attractive woman who had just walked out of the nearest house.

"McGraw—"

"She's not that bad. Really. Just get me through this, okay? And if I say we're leaving, we're leaving—no matter who's crying."

Rita didn't say anything else. He really knew how to reassure a person. He had it all worked out—so long as *he* was the one who wanted to leave. She wondered what the plan might be if *she* were the one crying and anxious to go.

"Okay?" he asked again.

"And then we're even, right?" Rita said. "This cancels out the tutoring."

He looked into her eyes. "Right. Except then, I'll owe you—"

"Here you are at last!" the woman cried as she opened the car door on McGraw's side. She was absolutely, beautifully, perfectly turned out—and well-preserved, as Sadie would say.

Mrs. McGraw waited impatiently for her son to get out, and she wasn't about to let Rita help. She nearly bowled him over when he was finally on his feet. He had to dig in with his crutches while she hugged him and kissed him and hugged him again. "I thought you'd never get here!"

"It's Rita's fault. She can't drive," McGraw said.

Rita gave him a pointed look, which he ignored. There was nothing for her to do but stand there.

McGraw finally extracted himself from his mother's grasp long enough to shake hands with his father.

"Mom and Dad, this is Rita Warren," he said, motioning for Rita to come closer.

"Ah, yes. Rita," his mother said, taking Rita in from head to toe in one sweep and smiling if it killed her.

Rita wondered idly what the "belt" she'd intended to wear would have done to that smile.

"Mr. and Mrs. McGraw," she said, stepping forward and extending her hand to Mr. McGraw, who was the closest.

"Rita, it's very kind of you to drive my son home. I know he appreciates it—regardless of what he just said. I hope you'll enjoy your stay with us. Have you ever been to Savannah before?"

"No," Rita said, surprised by the welcome and by the fact that her being here seemed perfectly acceptable to him. "But I read that book," she added mischievously.

Mr. McGraw laughed. "Well, if it's the book I think you mean, we have some serious correcting to do. If the lieutenant here feels up to it, maybe he can show you some of the *real* Savannah while you're here."

"Of course, he's not going to feel up to it," Mrs. McGraw said. "He's only just—"

"Lead on, my dear, lead on!" Mr. McGraw interrupted. "We've got some big-time welcoming home to do and not much time to do it in."

They went in through the kitchen and then down a wide hallway. The house was lovely inside. Bare wood floors, waxed over the years into a rich, warm patina, and accented with thick Oriental rugs. Rita looked around at the high ceilings, carved banisters, antique furniture. She could smell coffee and a spicy potpourri. Classical music—one of those little, random-sounding groups with a couple of violins and an oboe—played quietly in the background.

A china cabinet caught Rita's eye. It was full of porcelain dishes. She saw one of her favorite patterns among them, one the landlord had taken.

"Rita, are you coming?" Mrs. McGraw said, as if she thought Rita might try to steal something.

"I was just admiring the porcelain cups," Rita said.

Mrs. McGraw smiled. "Oh? Any in particular?"

"The 'Samarcande,' the blue, white and gold ones. I used to have some of those," Rita said, wondering if she'd just been given some kind of test.

McGraw made a point of waiting for Rita to catch up, a gesture she found both comforting and unsettling. Mrs. McGraw led the way, and Rita realized that McGraw had been right to dread this visit. The house ahead of them was full of people. It was standing room only in the living room, front hall and foyer. Rita felt no awkwardness per se—she'd been on too many stages and runways for that, but she would bless the moment she had decided to take

Corey's and Lou's fashion advice. Outwardly, at least, she belonged.

People were beginning to realize that McGraw had arrived. Rita had to stand back to let them press forward. He was swamped by well-wishers, for all intents and purposes, trapped. And he looked it. There was absolutely nothing she could do to help him.

"When will Joanna get here?" she heard someone ask him.

"I really don't know. I haven't spoken to her," McGraw answered.

"But she knew you were coming home surely?" his mother said, clearly alarmed by the possibility that there had been some breakdown in communication between the two.

"I can call her later," he said. "Right now, I want to show Rita her room. Where did you put her?"

Every one of the people standing with him turned and looked in Rita's direction.

"My dear, I do so admire you," the woman closest to her said.

"Because?" Rita asked, mystified. It was true that McGraw could be a horse's behind when it came to taking out his frustration on other people— if he could get away with it, but being able to ignore his bad moods was hardly cause for admiration.

"Because of your chosen work, of course. I really wanted to do the same thing when I was your age."

Rita looked at her, trying to understand. Try as

she might, she couldn't imagine this woman in feathers and beads.

"It's so…selfless," the woman said helpfully.

"Selfless," Rita said.

"Being a nurse. You are a nurse, aren't you? Isn't that why you made the trip with Mac?"

"Oh, heck, no," Rita said. "Actually, I'm an unemployed showgirl—from Las Vegas."

The woman looked startled, then smiled when she decided Rita must be joking.

McGraw was motioning impatiently for Rita to come with him, and she left the woman standing.

"I can take her up," his mother was saying. "I'm sure you don't want to tackle the stairs—"

"No, the stairs are no problem. I'm supposed to keep moving. You wouldn't believe the things they do to you if you don't."

"And that's exactly why you should have stayed in Texas, darling—"

"Don't go there, Mother, please. Rita?" he said, looking around for her. "Excuse me, everybody—"

Rita waited for him to take the lead. Naturally, that didn't suit him.

"That way," he said, pointing with a crutch.

She went first, but she had to keep stopping and waiting for him to talk to people along the way. It took forever to reach the stairs.

"You are such a hardhead," she said as he struggled slowly up each step. The crutches became a nuisance early on, and he had to hold on to the banister with one hand and her shoulder with the other. She carried the crutches.

"Did I lie? The doctors want me to do stuff like this."

"So, how are you planning to get back downstairs?" she couldn't resist asking anyway.

"I'm not if I can help it."

"Do you know all these people?"

"Every damn one of them," he assured her. "What was Mary Beth saying to you?"

"Mary Beth was admiring my career choice. She thought I was your private duty nurse."

"Yeah? What did you tell her?"

"The truth—now which way," she said, because they'd reached the top.

"Straight ahead."

He didn't take back the crutches. He leaned on her instead. Their ultimate destination was a large, airy room at the end of the hall. It had huge windows and a high ceiling, and it was sparsely furnished with a four-poster bed, an armless rocking chair, a dresser, and a tilting, full-length mirror on a stand. The rest of the room was all open floor space. She could have easily conducted a dance class in here.

McGraw took back his crutches, but he used them so he could sit on the edge of the bed. There was a large antique crib at the foot, one seemingly too big for just one baby. It was beautiful, the bed part of it nearly waist high but the railings low enough to reach over. She stared at it, thinking immediately of

Olivia and wondering how many McGraw infants had slept here.

"I need to rest a minute," he said. "And then we're going sight-seeing."

"We've already been sight-seeing."

"Okay, then. I'm going AWOL."

"Are you deliberately trying to upset your mother?" she asked.

"No, I'm trying *not* to upset me."

"What if Joanna comes and you're not here?"

"You mean, what if Joanna comes and I'm off someplace with you, don't you?"

Rita ignored the question. "You should call her."

"No," he said. "I shouldn't."

She didn't say anything else. She had no wish to get any closer to what he may or may not have seen in the hospital parking lot that day.

To her dismay, he lay back on the bed and stretched out.

"Warren, could you stop looking so worried?" he said.

"I don't see how. Every crazy thing you do while you're here is going to be *my* fault."

"Probably so," he agreed. But he made no move to get up.

"McGraw—"

Someone knocked quietly on the door. Rita stood there, with no intention whatsoever of opening it.

"Got to be Mama with the tar and feathers," McGraw said.

"That's not funny," Rita said.

"The longer you wait, the worse it looks," he warned her.

She sighed and went to open the door. It was indeed McGraw's mother. And McGraw's fiancée, who noted Rita's dress but who absolutely refused to look her in the eye.

"There you both are," Mrs. McGraw said brightly. "Look who's here, darling," she called to McGraw. "Rita, I guess we'll just have to give the lovebirds some privacy."

Rita glanced at McGraw and Joanna. They might be lovebirds, but they both looked more like deer caught in headlights.

The irrepressible Mrs. McGraw waited for Rita to step into the hall, then closed the bedroom door firmly after her.

"This way," she said, and began walking briskly away. Rita had little choice but to follow her. Halfway along the corridor, Mrs. McGraw opened the door to a small library or study.

"In here."

She stood back for Rita to precede her.

Rita went inside, but she couldn't resist a last look over her shoulder in the direction she'd just come. She was more concerned about whatever might be going on between McGraw and Joanna than she would ever have admitted.

"I want you to know something," Mrs. McGraw said immediately. "I am not fooled. I know exactly what you're up to." She looked at Rita as if she expected an immediate and very hot denial.

Rita stood with her hands behind her back and read the titles of some of the books on the shelves instead. "Yes," she said after a moment.

"Yes?"

Rita looked at her. "Yes, Mrs. McGraw. Yes, I'm trying to take advantage of your son. Yes, I know all about his money and his social position. Yes, it doesn't matter to me in the least that he's engaged. Yes, we're lovers. Yes, I take care of his sexual needs every chance I get. And yes, I know a lot of ways to put a great big smile on his face—"

"That's enough!"

"It is, isn't it? It sounds really awful when you just come right out and say it like that. But I did say it right, didn't I? I said exactly what you think."

"You seem to find this amusing, but I can assure you, I don't."

"Mrs. McGraw, you're getting way ahead of yourself here—"

"Oh, please. I know exactly the kind of woman you are. He's very vulnerable now, and what's left of him isn't going to be taken over by somebody like you."

"What's left of him? He's got a few scars—mental and physical ones—but he's going to be all right—"

"Oh, really? You don't know what he was like before. You don't know what it's like to have a child like him. There was nothing he couldn't do. Absolutely nothing. Sports, music, mathematics. Everybody—*everybody*—loved him—"

"Will you listen to yourself? He was hurt. He's not *dead*—"

"He was so handsome."

"He's still handsome, Mrs. McGraw."

"If he's married to Joanna—she can bridge the gap. People will know he's still himself if she's by his side. She can make him..."

"What?" Rita asked when the woman didn't go on. "Acceptable? I just don't understand people like you. I mean, really. If you're ashamed of him, then why do you go to all this trouble to put him on display for those people downstairs. What is *that* about?"

"You are not going to ruin his life," Mrs. McGraw said, ignoring the question. "I won't have it."

"You are so wrong about this. Your son and I are just—"

"Does he know about your past? Have you told him anything about that?"

"It never came up!"

"No, I didn't think so. Maybe we should go do that right now—"

"Fine!" Rita said. "Why don't we go do that!"

The door abruptly opened, and McGraw stood there, teetering on his crutches.

"What's going on?" he asked, looking from one of them to the other.

"Nothing," Rita said. She managed a smile. "Excuse me," she said, trying to get past him. He wouldn't move aside.

"Where are you going?"

"Your mother needs to talk to you," she said. She tried not to look at him, but he was waiting for her to do just that. She finally let her eyes meet his, but only briefly.

"Okay, what did you say to her, Mother?"

"I?" Mrs. McGraw said, feigning such surprise that Rita had to admire her. "Where is Joanna?" she asked, obviously adept at changing the subject, as well.

But McGraw refused to be sidetracked. "What did you say to Rita, Mother?"

"Oh, all right! I merely suggested that there were things you hadn't been told. Things Ms. Warren certainly should have told you."

"Things," he repeated. "You mean, like Joanna's new best friend?"

"Joanna's— I don't understand."

"I mean the guy who drives her up from Savannah whenever she comes to see me. The one who waits in the parking lot. The one she's so grateful to, she's all over him as soon as she gets back in the car."

"What are you talking about?" his mother cried.

"I'm talking about what *you're* talking about, Mother. The things Rita *didn't* tell me, and I couldn't agree more. She should have. She saw the two of them—just like I did—but she never said anything to me, not one word. I guess she thought I had enough to worry about—or maybe she thought it would hurt my feelings if I found out my fiancée had somebody on the side. The funny thing is that Joanna thought Rita did tell me. She was all ready to explain it all away—how mistaken Rita was about the whole thing. She was going to keep letting me think the marriage was still on, because—as she put it—she just felt so *sorry* for me.''

"Where is Joanna?" Mrs. McGraw asked again.

"Gone to tell whoever-he-is that she's a free woman."

"You haven't broken your engagement—"

"*She* broke the engagement, Mother. Not that she had much choice. And now I think you owe Rita an apology—"

"Oh, I think not," Mrs. McGraw said, folding her arms.

"Get out of the way, McGraw," Rita said, trying to get by him again. "I mean it." She'd had about enough of this.

He wouldn't move. "You and I are establishing some new coping mechanisms, Warren," he said. "I'm not going to throw things and you're not going to run."

He kept staring at his mother, waiting for the apology he must know would never come.

"Let's go," he said abruptly to Rita.

So much for coping mechanisms.

"McGraw, *I* want to go. You don't have to—"

"Are you going to keep to the plan or not?" he interrupted. "When I say go, we go. Now let's do it."

"McGraw—"

"Let's go, damn it!"

"All right!"

Mrs. McGraw didn't try to stop him, but that didn't keep her from following along. They went down the steep and narrow back stairs this time, and McGraw was in agony with every step.

"Aren't you going to speak to your father before you go?" his mother asked stiffly when they reached the back door. In any other circumstances Rita thought the woman might have asked—begged—McGraw to stay. But not with somebody like Rita Warren looking on.

"You speak to him, Mother. I'm sure you'll put a better spin on the situation than I would. None of this is your fault, right? My leaving has nothing to do with you jumping all over somebody who was supposed to be a guest in this house and who was doing me a damn big favor. Whatever you want to think, the bottom line is, I wouldn't have come home if Rita hadn't agreed to come with me."

"What is the matter with you!" Mrs. McGraw cried. "Can't you see what she is? This person— this woman—you think so highly of is nothing but a common—"

"Don't!" McGraw said, holding up one hand to stop her. "Mother, don't."

"She's not what you think she is!"

"Neither was Joanna."

Rita didn't wait to hear any more. Whatever Mrs. McGraw knew, she was going to tell sooner or later, and Rita didn't want to be there for it.

It was just beginning to rain, and she hurried across the back garden to her car. It was blocked in by two other vehicles. She got inside anyway. Even if she could only maneuver a millimeter at a time in each direction, even if it took pulling forward and backing up all night, she was leaving—with or without McGraw.

It was raining hard by the time she got the car free. He opened the door on the passenger side just as she was ready to back her way out into the street.

He didn't say anything when he got in, and neither did she. She just headed out, intending to find the right road without having to ask him anything. She glanced at him from time to time. He was wet and cold, but she knew better than to mention it. She had tried to tell him her coming along was a bad idea, and he just wouldn't listen.

Eventually she got them back on the interstate.

Now what? she wondered as she drove along.

Traffic was heavy in spite of the rain. He was beginning to shiver, and she reached to turn on the heater.

"Take the next exit," he said abruptly.

She looked at him. "Why?"

"Just do it."

She took the exit, thinking that perhaps he was sick. She didn't think for a moment that he had suddenly decided that he wanted her to drive him back to his parents' house. He motioned for her to pull into an abandoned service station.

"Stop here," he said.

She did, but she didn't understand. The rain beat against the roof of the car. She could barely see out the windows. He wasn't saying anything.

"McGraw, I'm sorry about Joanna."

"I don't want to talk about that. I want to…"

He reached for her, his arms sliding around her. He pulled her close to him, his head resting on her shoulder. She was startled at first, tentative, but then she put her arms around him, and he gave a shaky sigh.

"McGraw, I know you're upset."

"I'm not upset," he said.

"Even if you did see her and that guy in the parking lot, you still didn't *know*—not for sure. You were going to marry her, and she—"

"Don't talk, Warren. Don't explain it to me. I don't want to talk. I don't want to listen. Just let me be close to you. That's all I want."

She hesitated a moment, then tightened her arms around him. Without thinking, and in much the way she would have comforted Olivia, she pressed her cheek against his.

The wind and rain buffeted the car. Every now and then, a vehicle leaving the interstate went past.

After a moment he lifted his head to look at her, and he reached to stroke her face, to touch her mouth with his fingertips. Then he leaned forward. His mouth lightly brushed hers, so lightly she could barely feel it.

But it still took her breath away.

Her lips parted, and he kissed her then, a kiss she suddenly realized had been a long time coming. She clutched the back of his wet shirt and leaned against him in an effort to receive, to give in return. His tongue probed her mouth, and she gave a soft moan, savoring the feel and the taste of him. It had been so long since she'd kissed anyone, so long since she'd even wanted to kiss anyone.

McGraw…

She had never been kissed like this before. Never. She could feel his need, his desire, and something else…something so sweet…something she had been looking for all her life.

His fingers slid into her hair, raking her demure and ''delicate'' look into disarray. Her hair tumbled down around her shoulders, and he buried his face in it.

''McGraw…'' she said when he would have kissed her again. ''Wait—this is not what you need… Wait—''

''No,'' he said, his mouth finding hers.

''McGraw!'' she said, pushing against his chest.

She was afraid of herself, not him. She was so afraid of what she was feeling.

He stopped, his forehead resting against hers, his breathing ragged.

After a moment he moved away from her.

"Sorry," was all he said.

Chapter Ten

McGraw made the mistake of looking out his hospital window. Rita's car was still in the same place by the front entrance. He stood watching, expecting her to drive off any minute.

Go on, damn it. Go!

She didn't, and suddenly he couldn't stand it anymore.

"Hey!" he yelled at an orderly passing the door.

"Sir?"

"Come here. See that car down there. Get down there *now* and tell her to wait. Do *not* let her drive off."

"Yes, Sir!"

McGraw moved into the hall as quickly as he

could and headed for the elevators, forming the plan as he went. He would bring up the rear via the elevator, and then…

He didn't know what the hell he'd do then. He stood impatiently. Nothing was happening with the elevators.

"Come on, come on!" he said, pushing the button again and trying to will the doors to open.

One of the nurses caught sight of him. "Lieutenant McGraw?" she called down the hall.

"I'm not here!" he said.

"Right," she answered. "Where are you, then?"

"Savannah."

"Works for me," she assured him.

The elevator doors finally opened and he hobbled on, knowing he was going to look like one more damn fool if Rita had left in spite of his unsubtle attempt to keep her. Maybe he was reading way too much in the fact that she hadn't driven off like a bat out of hell. Maybe her car died.

She was still there when he struggled out the front doors, and so was the medic.

"Good job, soldier," McGraw said to him as he hobbled past.

"Too easy, Sir."

McGraw smiled slightly to himself. There was nothing easy about this woman. Absolutely *nothing*.

McGraw opened the car door and didn't hesitate about getting in. As usual, it took some doing, and he wasn't absolutely sure she wouldn't speed off with half of him still on the sidewalk.

But she waited, giving him plenty of time. Too much time.

He looked at her.

"I'm going to regret this," she said.

"No, you're not."

"Yes, I am," she said, starting the car. "And so are you."

The bad weather had followed them up from Savannah. Rita drove through the rainy darkness without telling him where they were going. He didn't care where they were going—literally or figuratively. He was just happy to be along for the ride.

He kept looking at her. Her hair had come all undone when he'd kissed her. She was so beautiful with it tumbling down her back like that. It was all he could do not to touch her.

She turned off the boulevard and onto a tree-lined side street, and still he didn't ask about their destination. She finally slowed and turned into a driveway next to a big, two- maybe three-story house that had apparently been cut up into several apartments. He could see a number of mailboxes on the wall near the front door.

She pulled as close to the rambling front porch as she could get, then rummaged in her purse and gave him a key.

"Second door on the left," she said. "I'm going to have to park around back."

He stuck the key into his shirt pocket, then managed to get out and maneuver up the steps without too much difficulty. The entrance hall was dimly lit and narrow. He made a lot of noise when he bumped his crutches into a chair and a small table as he tried to get by. Luckily, no tenants appeared to protest the racket. He unlocked the door to Rita's apartment and went inside, fumbling along the wall for a light switch.

He finally found it. It turned on a small lamp on the other side of the room. He looked around, not sure which way to go. The place was very neat and very impersonal. The message light on her answering machine was blinking.

He was still standing just inside the door when Rita came in.

"You're soaked," he said.

She smiled. "My grandmother used to tell me not to ever, *ever* get wet in the rain like this. You know why?"

"Why?" he asked.

"Because sugar melts."

He laughed, glad to see this Rita again, the one who offered him little tidbits of her life as if they were gifts she would only share with someone she trusted.

She was looking at him intently.

"What?" he asked.

"I don't even know your name."

"McGraw," he said. "Lieutenant First Class."

"Your *first* name."

"Boyd. And don't laugh."

"Boyd," she repeated. "But everybody calls you Mac."

"Right. Everybody but you."

They continued to stare at each other. Her lips parted slightly.

"There's more," he said abruptly. There had been nothing revealing about the dress she was wearing. Nothing. It was pretty enough, a lilac-colored, floaty…Joanna-kind-of-a-thing that had watercolor flowers on it. He couldn't even see her legs. But now it was wet, and she might as well have been standing there naked.

"So what comes after Boyd?" she asked.

"Tyree…and then Marshall,"

"Boyd Tyree Marshall McGraw," she said. "The Third?" she asked. She was smiling, but she seemed so…sad.

"The Fourth, actually. Rita, do you want me to leave or what?"

She came closer to him, and she was still looking at him so intently.

"Or what," she said.

She gave a quiet sigh. "How did we ever get here, McGraw?" she asked, her eyes searching his.

"I don't know," he said. "Rita, I just—"

She reached up to press her fingertips lightly against his lips.

"No, on second thought, I don't want to talk or

listen, either. This is just something we need, I guess. We've both got our scars, right? Us being together—tonight—doesn't mean anything. We aren't going to let it get in the way.''

"Rita," he began, but clearly she didn't want to discuss the matter.

"The bathroom is in there. The bedroom is in there. I'll be back in a minute.''

She left him and went into what he assumed was the kitchen. To do what? He had no idea. He thought he heard a back door close.

When she came back, he was waiting for her, standing by her bedroom door.

"Where did you go?" he asked.

"To let the neighbor's cat in out of the rain. Are you hungry?''

"No," he said, which wasn't quite the truth. He was hungry, but not for food.

He'd never quite been in this kind of situation before. He was certainly not a virgin, but in his experience, first-time lovemaking had never come out of a long-held, mutual need like this. She clearly had no intention of being coy, and looking at her now, he wasn't sure that it was going to be all that meaningless—at least, not on his part. On some level he must have known where they were heading, because he had made the effort to talk to Bugs today. He wanted to establish once and for all whether or not he was invading another man's territory. And Bugs had been forthcoming, his response both overt and subtle. He and Rita Warren didn't have a history. They were friends—period. And a certain officer had better not do anything to hurt her.

McGraw hobbled into the bedroom and sat on the bed. Rita took the crutches when he didn't know quite where to put them. The real truth of the matter was that he wasn't entirely sure he was physically able to do this. The best he could hope for was that that adage was true.

Where there's a will, there's a way.

He definitely had the will. Mentally at least, everything was "go."

It was still raining outside. Rita switched on the bedside lamp. It gave the room a kind of soft, golden glow. After a moment she turned her back to him and lifted her hair out of the way so that he could undo the long zipper in her dress. His fingers trembled. Had he ever approached any woman with this much anticipation? He didn't think so.

She stepped out of the wet dress. She was wearing some kind of slip underneath, lace and satin, see-through over her breasts and coming just to her thighs. She had a beautiful body, one she was not in the least self-conscious about. He couldn't stop staring.

She took the wet dress and went into the bathroom. In a moment he could hear water running and her humming. When she came back, she had on a flannel robe with little rosebuds all over it, and he could smell that old-fashioned scent again—the almond and cherries one he found so intoxicating. Her face had been scrubbed clean of makeup. She looked so young and vulnerable.

He watched her every move as she went around the room, putting things away, closing the blinds, turning down the other half of the bed—and she knew it.

"Do you need any help?" she asked.

"No," he answered.

She went away again, this time into the living room. He supposed that she wanted to leave him to his struggle to undress without an audience. He could hear her answering machine playing back her messages—all of them men's voices—and then music from the radio or the stereo, something not what he would have thought was her taste at all.

Rita abruptly turned off the music.

He hadn't made much progress by the time she came back. She sat beside him on the bed and reached around him to prop all the pillows against the headboard. When she straightened, she was very close to him and, after a moment, he leaned toward her so that he could lightly kiss her mouth. He was surprised somehow, regardless of her state of undress, that she let him do it.

How did they get here, indeed?

He put his arms around her. He loved the way she tasted—he had known that he would—but he didn't kiss her again. He just wanted to hold her.

"I'm glad," he whispered against her ear.

"About what?"

"I'm glad you didn't melt," he said, and she laughed.

"Well, the night is still young."

He leaned back so that he could look into her eyes.

"Maybe I...can't..."

"I want to spend the night with you, McGraw. I want to go to sleep with you and wake up with you—here. Beyond that..."

He didn't let her finish whatever else she intended to say. He kissed her, and the kiss escalated until she broke away. He was trembling with desire. She moved on her knees behind him to the head of the bed, making sure the pillows were in the right place when he slid back to join her.

He took off his T-shirt, forgetting the now-healed scars all over his torso until he saw her face. She didn't say anything at first. She moved closer to him, facing him, her hands resting lightly on his shoulders.

Then she leaned forward to nuzzle his cheek, to press a kiss at the corner of his mouth. "My poor McGraw," she whispered, looking into his eyes.

He had been so certain that he never wanted anyone's pity, and to get it now, from her, hit him hard. He had to look away.

She moved closer still, until she could kiss his mouth, so gently, again and again, and then more insistently until he gave a soft moan. His arms slid around her, and it became serious business then, kiss for kiss, touch for touch. He couldn't get enough of the taste and the feel of her.

He wanted more.

He slid his hands into the neck of her robe to caress her breasts. The robe parted—she was so beautiful.

"Tell me," he said. "Tell me you want me."

"I want you," she answered, and he believed her.

She had to help him, after all. He no longer minded anything she might do for him. She got him out of the only clothes he could wear these days— his uniform of the day—army-issue P.T. shorts, incongruous because he always looked as if he were dressed to go for his morning run, when he could barely walk. She was afraid she would hurt him, but he was too impatient to have her go slowly.

He brought her astride him, sliding the robe off her shoulders and letting it fall, pressing his face between her breasts. He couldn't wait. He entered her quickly, deeply. It was as if all his pent-up anger and frustration, guilt and sadness had been translated into fierce desire.

And no one—*no one*—could take care of him but her.

But he made the journey alone, with no thought of anything but the pleasure—*his* pleasure, and *his* need. He completely lost himself in the solace of her body.

He cried out at the end, and then he slumped

against the pillows, still holding her tightly, his breathing harsh and ragged against her shoulder.

"No," he managed to say when she would have moved away from him. He didn't want to let go of her. Not yet. He lifted his face to look into her eyes.

Did she know? Did she have any idea what she had done for him?

So good. It was so good!

"Sorry," he said. "I couldn't...wait for you—"

He kissed her mouth, her eyes, her mouth again, then buried his face in her neck, holding her close until he could finally bear to part with her. They lay quietly, side by side, with no sound except the rain.

His body was exhausted. He closed his eyes, but in his mind he kept seeing her, remembering bits and pieces of the times they had been together, the algebra, her grandmother's burned-out house, talking to the waitress at the barbecue joint. A hundred questions formed without his even realizing it, questions he couldn't ask, because this wasn't supposed to mean anything, and it most definitely wasn't going to get in the way.

He must have dozed. He opened his eyes to the sound of voices—Rita's and a man's. He sat up and struggled to get dressed.

"Corey's father is back in the hospital," he heard the man say. "She wanted to know if you'd take Olivia for tonight—until she can make some other arrangements."

"You know I will, Matt—" Rita said, or tried to.

"No, Rita, actually I don't."

"I'll take care of her. You can trust me."

The man laughed. "Corey is the one who trusts you—not me."

"That's not fair!"

"Isn't it? You left the kid twice, Rita. Twice."

"I left her with *you.*"

"Well, we can thank God for that, can't we? Or she'd be hanging out in casinos *and* topless bars."

"I did the best I could!"

The man was silent for a time. McGraw put on his shorts, then got up and moved to the only chair in the room, where he could see out the door.

"Yeah," the man said finally. "I think you probably did."

"You can leave her as long as you want."

"Well, we better not get into that," the man said. "Shorty, come here—" he called.

A little girl suddenly stood in the doorway, staring at McGraw.

"Boo!" she said, grinning.

"Come here, short stuff," the man said. "Give your old man a bye kiss—and look after Mama—"

The man froze at the sight of McGraw sitting there. Then he picked up the little girl and abruptly turned away.

"Matt, where are you going!" Rita cried.

The man didn't answer her. The door slammed. Hard. Outside, McGraw could hear it raining, hear a car leaving. Inside, the house was filled with one sound.

Rita Warren crying.

He hobbled into the living room. She was standing in the middle of the room, her head bowed.

''Rita?'' he said, crossing to her, holding on to the furniture, because he didn't take the time to get the crutches. ''Don't—don't—''

She looked up at him, and the moment he saw her face he knew how accurate her prophesy had been.

I'm going to regret this.

Chapter Eleven

McGraw took a taxi back to the hospital. There was nothing else he could do. Rita wouldn't talk to him, except to tell him to go. Basically, all he knew about the situation was what he had overheard.

He hadn't wanted to leave. He had wanted to stay and help her if he could. He wanted her to need him, the way he needed her. But she had meant what she said. Their being together for a night, or even part of a night, wasn't going to get in the way.

When he got off the elevator, he ran into the same nurse he'd encountered the last time he'd returned unexpectedly.

"Lieutenant McGraw," she said in surprise. "Here you are again—or are you?"

He didn't answer her.

"Your mother's been calling."

He didn't respond to that, either.

"That's what I was afraid of," she said.

He was emotionally and physically exhausted. He couldn't stop thinking about Rita, about making love with her, about the way she had looked when he left her.

He eventually went to bed, and he actually fell asleep, in spite of his mental turmoil, he supposed, because he'd had, by any standards, one hell of a day. He didn't wake up again until someone came to do the morning blood pressure and temperature check. Afterward, he decided to bite the bullet and call Rita. He was worried about her, and frankly, he didn't care if she knew it. There was so much he didn't understand, so much he wanted to know, and one of these days he was going to corner her into telling him everything. He let the phone ring until the answering machine picked up.

"Rita? If you're there, pick up. Rita—"

There was no answer.

Shortly after lunch he saw Doyle ride by the door—twice.

"Doyle!" he called the third time the soldier went by.

"Sir?"

"I...want to ask you something."

Doyle rolled his wheelchair as far as the open doorway. He'd been down this road already, and it

was obvious he wasn't exactly leaping at the chance
to make a return trip.

"This is personal," McGraw said. "You don't
have to answer."

"Sir, if it's about Rita again, I don't think I—"

"Who is Matt?"

"Matt, Sir?"

"He came to Rita's yesterday with a little girl.
Who is he?"

Doyle took a long time to make up his mind about
whether or not he wanted to give up anything.

"Staff Sergeant Matt Beltran, Sir. You called his
house the other night—"

"And the little girl?"

"That would be Shorty, sir. Olivia. She's Beltran's kid—and Rita's."

"They were married?" McGraw asked, feeling a
pang of what could only be described as jealousy
that Doyle knew the nickname of a child he hadn't
even known existed.

No, that wasn't quite true. He'd heard the name,
Olivia, before. The waitress at the barbecue place
had mentioned her. He himself had even asked about
it—and Rita had completely blown him off.

"Sir, no, Sir. They never got married."

Doyle backed out of the doorway, because one of
the orderlies had come to take McGraw to his scheduled dressing change.

"Sir," Doyle said around him. "If you want to

know anything else, I think you'd better ask Rita, Sir.''

Except that she won't tell me anything, McGraw thought.

The dressing change was hell. He had thought the last one was bad. He tried to keep his mind occupied by sorting through what he had just learned. Rita wasn't divorced. Rita wasn't married. Rita had a pretty little kid named Olivia-slash-Shorty.

''You've got some fever today,'' the doctor said. ''And you've still got that place on both burn sites.''

''What place?'' McGraw said, because this was the first he'd heard of it.

''We're going to have to watch that,'' the doctor said, ignoring the inquiry.

McGraw was of the opinion that he wouldn't be having to watch anything if they hadn't tried to kill him the last time his dressings were changed, but for once he kept quiet.

And the doctor was serious about keeping watch. McGraw had his temperature checked two more times by early afternoon. After supper, one of the nurses started an IV antibiotic. He felt like hell, and Rita still wasn't answering her phone.

He slept for a time. When he opened his eyes, Doyle was there.

''Have you talked to Rita?'' McGraw asked without prelude.

''Sir, no, Sir. I just came in to tell you I can't get hold of her. I think she's taken off again, Sir.''

"Taken off?"

"Sir, she does that when she's...upset. I guess that's what she is—if Beltran came to the apartment while you were there. Upset, Sir."

McGraw didn't say anything. He already knew about that particular way Rita had of dealing with her problems, and she had been *way* past upset.

"Do you have any idea where she would go?"

"Sir, no, Sir. Sir, I..."

McGraw waited for him to go on. He didn't.

"Say it, Doyle," McGraw said finally.

"Sir, Rita's had a rough life. She don't expect much in the way of help from nobody. You know that stuff they talk about in the family support group meetings."

"What stuff?" McGraw had had no occasion to attend any of the meetings, and he wouldn't have thought Doyle would have, either.

"All that stuff about human beings in crisis, Sir. Well, that's what Rita was before. A human being in crisis."

"And?"

Doyle looked at him. "Sir, one thing for sure. Ain't nothing more important to Rita than her kid."

McGraw got the message loud and clear. Doyle didn't mean "nothing." He meant "nobody." He meant Lieutenant Boyd T. M. McGraw.

After Doyle left, McGraw made a different phone call, and this time he left a message. Several messages. He got results much sooner than he expected.

Two hours later a soldier stood in the doorway. And the man was using everything he had to stay in the zone of military correctness.

"Sergeant Beltran?" McGraw guessed. It wasn't the Beltran he'd hoped for, but he'd have to make do.

"Sir, I've come to ask you a question," Beltran said, cutting to the chase.

"What is it?"

"I want to know why you're leaving phone messages for my wife."

McGraw looked at him. "I'm leaving them because I don't know what else to do—I don't know where Rita is." He stopped to give the sergeant an opportunity to volunteer her whereabouts, but he had nothing to say about that.

"I'm also leaving them because of what you said," McGraw said.

"What *I* said?"

"You said your wife—Corey—trusted Rita. I was thinking maybe it went both ways. Maybe she'd have some idea about where Rita had gone."

"She doesn't—Sir."

"I'd still like to talk to her," McGraw said.

"I don't think that will be possible, Sir," Beltran said.

They stared at each other.

"Sir, her father is in the hospital with another heart attack," Beltran said finally. "I'd just as soon she didn't have something else to worry her."

"Would you at least ask her if she knows where Rita would go?"

"Sir, nobody knows that but Rita."

The sergeant turned to leave.

"Beltran," McGraw said. "Your...little girl. She would have been all right with Rita and me."

The sergeant didn't say anything, regardless of how much he wanted to. After he had gone, McGraw slept again. When he woke, an envelope addressed to him lay on the bedside table. His mother had sent it via Express Mail from Savannah. He reached for it, curious about what she could possibly be up to now.

He had to struggle to get the thing open, because of the IV. When he finally got the end pulled apart, several pictures fell out. He picked them up and looked at them, one by one, then shoved them back into the envelope.

The light on the answering machine was blinking when Rita finally returned to the apartment, but it took her a long time to listen to the messages. She was still on the edge, still not sure where she belonged. Did she belong back in the clubs on the boulevard? Or did she belong here, pretending to be the woman Sadie Warren always said she could be? She had been gone nearly a week, and she was still no closer to knowing.

She took a deep breath before pushing the play button.

"Rita?" McGraw's voice said. "If you're there, pick up. Rita—"

Her eyes filled with tears. She sat on the corner of the couch. She had spent the last six days convincing herself that she didn't feel anything for him, and all she had to do was hear his voice to come undone.

She wiped her eyes and concentrated on the next message. It was the real estate agent with the property owner's terse reply to her offer—thanks, but no thanks—and an earnest recommendation that she bite the bullet and pay the rent the man was asking.

"Thanks, but no thanks," Rita murmured.

So now what? she thought. But she knew. She had to talk to Matt. She gave a quiet sigh. How could she make Matt understand her relationship with McGraw when she didn't understand it herself? Sending McGraw away had been one of the hardest things she'd ever done, but she had known that she had to be strong. She had wasted too much of her life already looking for some man's shoulder to cry on. She had to stand on her own two feet, if she was ever going to be whole.

It would have been so easy to let him take care of her. He had wanted to give her whatever she needed. She had seen it on his face. But she was perfectly aware that letting him stay would have meant answering his questions. The simple truth was that she was too ashamed of her past to let him get any closer, no matter how much she needed him.

She didn't want McGraw to ever know the details of her life before she'd met him or why Matt had been justified in saying what he'd said and thinking what he'd thought.

And poor little bewildered Olivia. She hadn't understood the sudden change in plans, but she had blown Rita a kiss as her father carried her out the door.

"Rita—" Bugs's voice said on the answering machine, jarring her back into reality. "Call me, baby, will you?"

The machine beeped.

"Rita—" his voice said again. "Call me as soon as you get in."

Then, the last message. "It's six o'clock— Wednesday night. I need to talk to you."

She frowned and stopped the machine. She didn't want to talk to Bugs now—she wanted to see Olivia. But she made the call. It took a long time for somebody to answer the phone, and the person who answered seemed to have no idea where Bugs Doyle might be.

Rita drove to the Beltran house. Matt's car was in the drive, but she stopped anyway, dreading crossing swords with him again. He opened the front door before she was halfway up the walk, and he had that look again, the one that told her she was the last thing he wanted to see on the doorstep.

"How's Olivia?" Rita asked, determined not to cower.

"Where the hell have you been?"

"I repeat. How is Olivia?"

"Olivia is fine—"

"And Corey's father?"

"He's home from the hospital—and you know what? Whatever this is, I don't want to deal with it."

"Well, that's tough—"

"Where have you been!"

"The Grand Strand mostly—"

"Myrtle Beach?"

"That's the one."

"What were you doing at Myrtle Beach?"

"I was looking for a job—if you must know."

"Doing what? Dancing in a club?"

"Why not? It's the one thing I do really well."

He didn't say anything. He just shook his head.

"What is it with you, Matt? Okay. I took off—again. But I didn't stay, did I? Tomorrow is my regularly scheduled visit. I didn't miss it. I'm not making any apologies here. I care about Olivia—you know that. And I care about McGraw. Somebody should have called first—and that's all I've got to say about it!"

He gave a sharp sigh. "So did you get a job?" he asked pointedly.

"Actually, I got three jobs...if I want them—and—"

"Rita," he interrupted. "People are looking for you."

"Why?"

"Didn't you call Bugs? I know he left messages on your answering machine."

"I tried to call him, but nobody knew where he was—"

"He's in intensive care."

"What? What's wrong with him?" Rita asked, alarmed now.

"Nothing. It's not him. It's McGraw."

"What's wrong with McGraw!"

"You mean besides worrying about where the hell you got to? He had to have surgery on his legs Tuesday night—I don't know what went wrong. He's in intensive care. Bugs has been sitting with him most of the time. They're the only two left and Bugs isn't leaving him. Just go to the hospital, okay? And try not to annoy his mother."

Rita stood there, unmoving.

"Rita," Matt said, "I think the guy needs you. Go."

Chapter Twelve

Rita could feel the animosity the moment she stepped off the elevator. Both Mr. and Mrs. McGraw were standing in the corridor. Mrs. McGraw's glance swept over her, head to toe.

Rita's chin went up. She had made a point of arriving in all her glory—her total, unabashed Rita self. She had on a tight, shiny black skirt—not a "belt" by Corey Beltran's standards, but no less provocative—and a skimpy, genuine silk, snake-print T-shirt, and her open-toed black ankle-strap high heels. She'd tied a small, red-print kerchief around her neck and carried a red-and-white fake patent leather bag. Her hair was "messy-chic," haphazardly caught up in a Pebbles Flintstone-sans-the-bone on top of her head.

"What are you doing here?" Mrs. McGraw asked without prelude.

"Hello, Mrs. McGraw," Rita said sweetly. "Mr. McGraw."

"What are you doing here?" Mrs. McGraw repeated, and her husband put his hand on her arm.

"I'm…here to see Bugs," Rita said impulsively.

"Oh, that's right," Mrs. McGraw said. "You and he were…special friends."

"The key word here being 'friends,' Mrs. McGraw."

"You lived with him, Ms. Warren," the woman said, clearly needing to show off how well-informed she was on the subject of Rita Warren.

"Yes. But Bugs and I never did the deed. I'd put my hand in the fire for him and I don't care who knows it—but I didn't do what you're thinking just to have a roof over my head—"

Rita suddenly didn't want to waste time antagonizing McGraw's mother or justifying her relationship with Bugs. What would somebody like her know about it? It suddenly occurred to Rita that probably the worst thing that had ever happened to this woman—except for her son joining the army—was Rita Warren.

She stepped to the nearest window. She could see McGraw without difficulty. He was lying there, surrounded by IV's and machines, his eyes closed. Bugs sat in a wheelchair next to the bed. She immediately understood the scenario. A Ranger never leaves a fallen comrade, dead or alive.

Mr. McGraw came to stand beside her.

"How is he?" she asked, glancing in his direction.

"Well, he's awake sometimes now—for a little while. I think he knows who we are—and where he is. But..."

She looked at him. "But what?"

"I'm afraid he hasn't asked for you."

Rita chose not to respond to that remark, mostly because she believed him.

"Can I get in to see him?" she asked anyway.

"Only if he wants you there."

She gave a wry smile. And she could crawl over Mrs. McGraw's dead body.

Bugs noticed her then, and he immediately rolled his wheelchair toward the door. Rita left Mr. McGraw standing to go hold the door open for Bugs to come out into the corridor.

"Where the hell have you been?" he asked immediately.

"Answering that same question mostly," she said. "What happened to him, Bugs?"

"Infection in the burns—like I had. Only the first antibiotic didn't work. They took him to surgery to try to clean up the places, and then he had some kind of reaction to a drug or something. And the antibiotic they're using now hasn't kicked in. They don't know if it'll work or not."

She didn't say anything. She'd been in this situation before—when Olivia had scarlet fever—waiting, praying for somebody to find an antibiotic that would work. She'd been so scared then, and she was scared now.

"Rita?"

She looked at him, but he didn't go on.

"What?" she said. "Tell me."

"One of the guys in the five-oh-four..." Once again, he left her hanging.

"Bugs, you're scaring me here. What is it?"

"Aw, this guy...he told me that a couple of weeks ago the word was out."

"What word?"

"Somebody was looking to buy pictures—of you—when you were doing the 'Ready Rita' thing at the club. He said one of his buddies got damn good money for the ones he had."

Rita frowned. "Who would want—" She glanced toward where Mrs. McGraw stood. She didn't have to ask that question.

"Has...McGraw seen them?"

Bugs didn't answer her, and he wouldn't meet her eyes. Of course McGraw had seen them, Rita thought. That was why Bugs was telling her this— so she'd understand when McGraw didn't want anything else to do with her.

She looked at Mrs. McGraw again. The thing she had so dreaded had happened.

You win, lady, Rita thought.

She walked to where she could see McGraw again through the window. He hadn't moved. She watched him for a long time, remembering his touch, his taste. She would never forget what it had been like with him. Never.

He opened his eyes for a moment. She couldn't tell if he was actually seeing her or not.

Yes, she could. He knew she was there. The look held, then he turned his face away.

"I'll see you later, Bugs," Rita said abruptly. She had to get out of here.

"Where are you going?"

"Home," she said over her shoulder. "If I can find one."

She impulsively came back and bent to kiss him on the cheek, then she forced a smile. "Don't let the bear eat you—or him, okay?"

Mr. and Mrs. McGraw stared at her as she approached, but she didn't say anything to either of them.

"What did Specialist Doyle say?" Mrs. McGraw asked as Rita walked past.

"He said you paid too much for the pictures," Rita answered.

McGraw made a halfhearted attempt to open his eyes again. They hurt. Everything hurt. Turning his head didn't help. He had no idea where he was. Not on the Black Hawk. Texas? No, he'd left Texas and Rita was at the window...

He gave a heavy sigh.

"Darling, are you awake?" his mother's voice said. "Mac?"

He opened his eyes for real this time and looked at her. And he remembered.

"Too…late," he said.

"What, darling?"

"Too late, Mother. You should have…sent me the pictures…*before* I…loved…her…"

Rita spent the day with Olivia at the Beltran house. It rained all afternoon. They watched the "P'Pan" movie twice, and then moved on to the mermaid.

Corey went out for a while. Olivia was napping when she returned, and Rita wandered into the kitchen where Corey was putting away groceries.

"So, how's your father?" Rita asked.

"He's better. Olivia had him coloring pictures with her yesterday. I think she's good medicine for him."

Me, too, Rita thought.

"You want to talk?" Corey asked, and Rita shook her head.

"Funny," Corey said. "I could have sworn you did."

"You don't know everything," Rita said, and Corey smiled.

"I know about being in love with somebody

when you know there's no way it's ever going to work and people think you're crazy.''

"Corey, the whole thing is crazy. I feel like I've been left at the altar, when nobody's ever said anything about loving anybody. McGraw and I didn't have any kind of big thing going. It was just…me.''

"You what?''

"Me being *me*. I never get it. The punch line always goes right over my head.''

"The punch line being?''

"No way, no how,'' Rita said.

"He was upset when he didn't know where you were,'' Corey said, putting a carton of eggs in the refrigerator.

"Was he?'' Rita asked, surprised.

But the spark of hope that flared at that revelation abruptly died.

"That was before,'' Rita said.

"Before what?''

"Before he found out about 'Ready Rita.'''

"Well, you should have told him about that before somebody else did.''

"No, I shouldn't. We weren't…*together*. We weren't even going in the same direction.''

"Yes, you were. It was obvious.''

"Was not.''

"Was, too,'' Corey said.

"His mother hates me.''

"Well, of course she does.''

"Gee, thanks, Corey. Why don't you really cheer me up?"

"My job isn't cheering you up. My job is listening."

"You could have fooled me."

"So what if she does hate you, Rita? She loves her son. Maybe she loves him enough to cut you some slack."

"No, it's more like she loves him enough to put a price on my head. None of this matters anyway. I wouldn't care about her if he—"

"If he what?"

"It doesn't matter," Rita said again. "McGraw doesn't want anything else to do with me."

Unfortunately she couldn't say the feeling was mutual. Twice she went to the hospital in the middle of the night, just to stand briefly again at the window and look at him. He never knew she was there. She still talked to Bugs. Every day. But he didn't have much to tell her except that McGraw was "holding his own."

But then the medical reports abruptly got better. McGraw had been "moved out of intensive care." McGraw was able to be "up and around again." And finally, "McGraw's gone home to Savannah."

Rita tried to stay busy. One Saturday, when she had brought Olivia to her apartment for the afternoon, someone knocked on her door. She thought it was Corey, and she opened the door with Olivia in her arms.

McGraw stood on crutches in the hallway.

"Hi, Mac!" Olivia said, astounding Rita even more.

"Hi, Olivia," he said. He had lost weight. His face was thin, but it was healed now. The scarring was there, but she didn't find it disturbing and never had. He'd had a new haircut and he looked so boyish and…wonderful.

"We met at the party last week," McGraw said. "A pizza party for the kids of the guys who were killed on the Black Hawk. Bugs and I went. Corey and Olivia were there helping—weren't you, short stuff?"

"Yes!" Olivia said.

"We kind of hit it off," McGraw said.

Rita kept looking at him, her disbelief mounting.

"So…can I…come in?" he asked after a moment.

Rita stood back, still more or less speechless, and let him hobble past.

"I thought you were in Savannah," she said finally.

"Well, you know how that goes," he answered.

"You're not taking medical retirement?"

"Not unless I have to," he said.

"Good," she said.

He looked at her. "Good?"

"Well, you shouldn't give up—if that's what you want."

"Right," he said. "So my old drill sergeant used to tell me."

He sat on the couch. Olivia immediately wanted down, and she cornered him with her new book. Rita stood watching them with their heads together.

"McGraw."

"What?" he said, looking up.

"What are you doing here?"

"Well, you wouldn't make the trip."

"Why would I do that?"

"Oh, I don't know. To see how I am, maybe. It's not like we're total strangers."

"Bugs told me how you were."

"We have unfinished business, Rita."

No, we don't, she thought.

She had nothing she wanted or needed to say to him. He'd seen the pictures and that was that. She hadn't set out to deceive him. She had made it clear from the beginning that her past was something she didn't talk about—wouldn't talk about. And even he would agree, with good reason.

She kept watching him with Olivia. They must have really bonded at the pizza party, she thought, because he was completely comfortable with her. She suddenly smiled at the running narrative he was giving about a particular page in the book. She doubted seriously that there was a Ranger bee in there who said "Hoo-ah!" every time the flowers popped up.

Maybe she did want him to know the truth, she

thought suddenly, and not his mother's edited version of it. Maybe she wanted to look him in the eye after all and just tell him.

This is what I am. Take it or leave it.

He would leave it, of course, but she would have the satisfaction of setting the record straight.

Someone knocked at the door again, and Rita went to answer it.

This time it was Corey.

"Well, this is a surprise," Corey said quietly, looking past Rita to where McGraw and Olivia were sitting.

"Tell me about it," Rita said.

"Hello, Lieutenant," Corey said. "Let's go, Olivia, hurry, hurry. Tell Lieutenant McGraw bye."

"Bye-bye, Mac," Olivia said, hopping down from the couch. "Be the good boy."

"Bye, Olivia," he answered, smiling. "Thanks for reading to me."

"Okay," Olivia assured him. "Bye, Mama," she said, lifting her arms to Rita.

Rita picked her up and kissed her noisily on both cheeks, making her giggle. "Love you."

"Love you," Olivia echoed. "Be the good girl."

"I will if you will," Rita said.

"I will if you will," Olivia answered.

"Good luck," Corey whispered on the way out. "Nice to see you again, Lieutenant," she called to McGraw.

The apartment was suddenly too quiet with Olivia gone.

Unfinished business, Rita thought. She stood for a moment before she turned to face McGraw.

"So, what's new?" she asked, throwing the door wide open for him.

"Not much," he answered easily. "How's the algebra?"

"I...missed a few classes."

"Well, you can catch up, right?"

"Yeah, I can catch up."

She moved to the chair across from him and sat. The conversation abruptly lagged.

"Rita, I'm not saying what I want to say—"

"Are you all right now?" she interrupted.

"You know I'm not. I'm trying to do what you wanted. I'm trying to pretend being with you—making love with you—didn't mean anything."

He was looking at her so intently. It was all she could do to hold his gaze.

"McGraw, what do *you* want?"

"I want you to tell me," he said, and she knew exactly what he meant. "Everything. Things you've never talked about to anybody. I don't want any more surprises."

She looked away. She knew exactly what "surprise" he meant, too.

"It's not going to work any other way, Rita."

"There's nothing between us to work or not work—"

"Tell me, damn it! I need to know!"

"Why! So you can decide whether or not you can live with it?"

"Yes," he said simply.

"And if you can't?"

"Then we're no worse off than we are now, are we?"

She gave a wavering sigh. If she wasn't very careful here, she was going to cry, and that was the last thing she wanted to do.

"After your grandmother died," he prompted, "you lived with your mother and the boyfriend of the week…"

"There's really no point in doing this," she said. "I don't need your acceptance or your approval."

"There's every point, Rita. Go on. You had the teacup—the one Bugs told me about. The one with the cameo in the bottom. Is that right?"

She looked at him, wondering what else Bugs had told him.

"Is that right?" he insisted.

"Yes!" she whispered fiercely. "That's right. I had the teacup—and that's all I had. One lousy teacup! I lived with people who didn't care about anything, not even themselves. And what a surprise, I turned out just like them."

"No, you didn't. Go on. You went to school. You were a good student…and then…"

"I *was* a good student," she said abruptly. "In spite of my family situation. Sadie believed in me and I held on to that. Until the middle of my senior year. Then everything just…fell apart. His name was Jo-Jo. Well, that wasn't his real name, but that was all the name my mama could get out of him. Boyfriend Number…who knows? I'd lost count by then. He…kept after me and after me. He wouldn't leave me alone, so I took off—my first real success at solving my problems by running away from them.''

Tears were running down her cheeks; she wiped them away with her fingers.

"I quit school. I had nowhere to go. But I thought I could get a job and everything would be okay. I was so stupid. Nobody will hire you when you don't know how to do anything. I couldn't make enough money to *live* on. My grandmother Sadie's house was empty then. My father had sold it as soon as the estate was settled, but whoever bought didn't want to live in it. Anyway, I broke into the house— Sadie was forever locking herself out, so I knew how to do it—and I stayed there for a while. Tino and Earlene—from the barbecue place—they caught me stealing food out of their Dumpster. They more or less took me in and gave me a job waitressing. But I…'' She shrugged. "I got to thinking there had to be more to life than slinging barbecue—and if I could just get some money, I could find out what.

"A girl at the Laundromat told me one of the clubs, where all the soldiers go, was looking for dancers. I can dance, McGraw. I really can. Ever

since I was little. You know how some people play
the piano by ear? Well, that's the way I can dance.
I can watch somebody and I can hear the beat—the
number of steps—in my head—and I can do them.
I thought I'd just go work in a club for a while—
make some good money—and then I'd go back to
school or something.'' She smiled. ''Tino and
Earlene had a fit—but I was kind of a hardhead.''

''Now there's news,'' he said. ''Go on.''

''It was so *bad,* McGraw. Me half naked and all
these drunk guys yelling things at me. I was so
scared—'' She gave a heavy sigh. ''This old guy in
the band. He told me if I needed money bad enough
to do this then I had better get myself together or
I'd be doing worse. 'Don't think about them men,
child,' he said. 'They ain't even here, if you don't
want them to be. Think about the music. Listen to
the music. *Dance* to the music. Let it carry you
where you want to go.'

''So that's what I did. I listened to the music and
I danced and I put everything else out of my mind.
And the funny part was, the more I showed those
guys they couldn't reach me, the more they wanted
to come and see me. I was 'Ready Rita'—but I was
so arrogant I wouldn't even give them the time of
day. All of a sudden, I was *the* sexual fantasy, the
woman who was so hot and so cold all at the same
time—''

Rita didn't say anything else. She could feel Mc-
Graw looking at her.

"Tell me about Beltran," he said finally, and she shrugged.

"Nothing to tell. Not really."

"Right. If you don't count a kid and the fact that you love him."

"Loved," she said after a moment. "He was kind to me, and I was starved for kindness. I was into collecting teacups by then. Funny, right? Somebody like me doing that. I was...trying to hold on to Sadie, I guess. Matt brought me one from Italy after he was stationed there—a real Sevres. He said orphans had to look after each other. I told him I wasn't an orphan. He said I was—he knew an orphan when he saw one. And he was right. I was orphaned the day my grandmother died. But he was just being kind, you know? Because that's the way he is. And then...a good friend of his got killed—he was taking Matt's place as jumpmaster on a training exercise. They'd been through basic training together and jump school and all that. Matt was all messed up about it. One night he was in the club and he was really drunk and looking to get hurt. I took him home with me so he wouldn't get picked up or worse. And we..."

She sighed again.

"He didn't even remember it. I didn't tell him I was pregnant. I knew he didn't love me or anything. I tried so hard to look after Olivia—she's beautiful, you know? And I couldn't do it. And then the landlord evicted us...he kept everything I had—"

"Sadie's teacup," McGraw said.

"Yeah. I didn't have anywhere to go. I had a hungry baby. I'd had this idea, see, for a long time. I thought about going to Las Vegas when they had the open auditions—they have them twice a year— and trying to get into one of those big shows. The classy ones, not the sleazy ones. I was tall enough and everything. I never did drugs and I wasn't too big in the wrong places. You'd think they'd want women with big breasts, but they don't. I figured I had chance, at least, to make a lot of money quick, and then Olivia and I would be set. If I could just get there—"

She stopped, and she looked into his eyes. "I think I must have been crazy. But I left her, McGraw. I left Olivia. I knew Matt was in the building and I put her in his car. I waited until some people came by, and I told them to tell him it was his turn now. And then I waited until I knew she was with him, and I—I left."

She had to wipe her eyes again. "I knew he'd take care of her and he did. That worked out pretty good. Matt and Corey—Corey was Olivia's foster mother—they have a good marriage and they've made a good home for Olivia. She's really happy with them. I can see that. I even like Corey. I tried not to, but you know how she is. She's so...*likeable.*

"So they were married and I still wasn't any better off financially. Matt got custody. I got visitation. I couldn't stand it, so I took off again. I finally went to Vegas. Bugs loaned me the money to get there. He said, 'You got to do something, baby—even if it's wrong.'

"But I made the cut at the audition. I got a job— *the* job, McGraw. It was so *great*—for a while. I was making really good money…doing what I loved to do—and I didn't have to take my top all the way off." She smiled. "I was a real, honest-to-god show-girl—beads and feathers, skimpy but tasteful. Even Sadie could have come and watched me.

"I was living the big dream, right? But I missed my baby. I just couldn't run away anymore, so I came home. I've been trying to make things right, trying to get myself straightened out. I don't want to upset Olivia's life, but I want her to know who I am and not…mind. It hurts so much to hear her call me mama when it doesn't mean anything to her. Corey is her mother, not me—"

She was crying again. She couldn't help it.

Mac was looking at her, and he wasn't saying anything. She wiped her eyes with the backs of her hands, then abruptly stood up and went into the kitchen, running away the way she always did. She could hear him coming after her, every step of his painful progress through the hallway into the kitchen.

She turned to face him.

"So, how did you like it, McGraw? The Ballad of Ready Rita Warren. Are you shocked or what? Your mother is just going to love it—"

"Don't," he said.

She took a step backward, bumping into the sink, but he kept coming. When he was close enough, he let the crutches fall and reached for her. She tried to hold herself stiff as his arms enfolded her, but he was warm and strong, and he was McGraw.

It doesn't mean anything, she thought wildly. *It doesn't.*

"McGraw—"

"Hush," he said. "Let me hold you. It may not make you feel better, but it does wonders for me."

She returned his embrace then, clinging to him as hard as she dared. He pressed a kiss against her cheek.

"We're standing on the edge of something here," he said. "You know that."

"No, I don't know that. It wouldn't work with us, McGraw. How could it? Even if you weren't who you are and I wasn't who I am, there's Olivia—"

"Hush," he said again.

He bent his head to kiss her, so softly at first, so sweetly, and she couldn't keep from responding. It was like finally coming home to one of those places she always dreamed about when she was a little girl. The house with flowers on the porch and love inside.

A fairy tale.

She didn't believe in them.

"It's not going to work," she said, breaking away and pressing her face into his shoulder.

He leaned back to look at her. "No," he said. "It's not. Not now. But we've got a chance—"

"A chance? McGraw, weren't you listening to me? Whatever you're feeling, it's not real. It's because of what happened to you. It's all tangled up with me being Bugs's friend and the two of you being the only ones left standing. And you're on the rebound from Joanna—it's some kind of any-port-in-a-storm thing—"

"Rita, you're not a port. If anything, you're the storm."

"What are you going to do when somebody makes some kind of remark about me—and believe me, sooner or later, they will."

"Military or civilian?" he asked without missing a beat.

"I'm serious!"

"So am I. I was listening. I heard every word. But nothing you said changes the way I feel about you. Seeing the pictures didn't change it—much to my mother's dismay. I've had nothing but time on my hands these past few weeks. All I've thought about is you. You're strong and you're real and you're what I need. I can't tell you how much I admire the person you are. I have from the very first—even when you were throwing a magazine at me."

"McGraw—"

"We've got a chance, damn it! But I have to have time."

Her eyes searched his. She wanted to believe him.

She gave a quiet sigh. "Time. Tell me what that means."

"The last thing you need is another messed-up paratrooper to keep straight," he said. "I want to be more to you than that. I love you, and I can't—" He looked away for a moment, then back at her. "I've lost who I am. I'm not any use to myself or anybody else. I have to find out how far I can come back—*if* I can come back. And I have to do it alone. Do you understand? You said you'd been trying to get yourself straightened out. Well, I have to do that, too. I know I don't have the right to ask you to wait or anything else. I don't even know how long it's going to take."

"McGraw, did you mean what you said?"

"About what?"

"You said you…loved me."

"I do. What did you think?"

"What did I *think?* We didn't exactly have a pleasant parting, now, did we? Then you saw those pictures…and I don't hear anything else from you. What could I possibly think?"

"That it threw me—the pictures and Matt Beltran. That maybe I needed a little time to get over it, not to mention to get out of intensive care. That as soon as I could, I'd come here."

She moved away from him.

"Rita, I love you with all my heart. I tried not to, but I—you'd better tell me now if it's one-sided, because I didn't think it was. When we made love—''

He stopped, and she looked at him.

She wanted so much to believe that maybe they really did have a chance, and that it was just a matter of needing time. She had plenty of that, and she had plenty of love. She *loved* him. That was the only thing in this situation she was certain about.

''It's not one-sided,'' she said.

But all the insecurities suddenly came back again.

''I can't even do algebra.''

He frowned. ''What?''

''I can't do algebra!''

''Rita, there are thousands and thousands of men on the post here. You and I could go right now and ask every damn one of them and they'd all say the same thing. None of them—*none* of them—ever wanted a woman because of her algebra!''

She couldn't keep from smiling. ''You think?''

''Yes, I think,'' he said, laughing and hugging her to him. ''I am so crazy about you! Now, will you answer the question? Are you going to give us a chance? Will you wait for me?''

She moved so that she could see his face.

''Yes,'' she said. ''And no.''

''Rita—''

''I'll give us a chance. But whatever you have to do to get better, you're not shutting me out. You're taking me along.''

''No—''

"I've already seen you at your worst, McGraw. I'm not going to be shuffled off to keep the home fires burning or wait by the window until you've decided you're all you can be. I mean it. I have to learn to live with your scars, you have to learn to live with mine. If we both have to dodge magazines to do it, I don't care. That's the deal."

He didn't say anything. He hobbled over to the table and pulled out a chair so he could sit.

"You still don't get it, do you?" Rita asked. "Even after you've seen the pictures. Even after everything I've told you. I love you, too, but I'm not Joanna. I come with a lot of baggage, McGraw. I have a real history here. But if you love me, starting right now, you're going to have to deal with it—all the time. Forever. No matter what else is going on. Just like I'll have to deal with thinking I'm not good enough. You're going to have to worry about whether or not it's going to get to be too much for me and maybe I'll pick up all that baggage and run—again. And I'll have to worry that you're going to look at Joanna one day and be sorry you ever hooked up with somebody like me—"

"Rita—"

"No, I mean it. That's the deal. Take it or leave it."

He looked at her a long moment.

"Hand me my crutches, will you? I want to be on my feet when I say this."

She picked up the crutches and handed them to

him, then stood back as he struggled to get out of the chair.

But even after he was standing, he still didn't say anything. She kept looking at him, waiting, expecting the only thing she could expect.

The absolute worst.

He took a quiet breath, and then he smiled. The smile was all she needed.

"Okay, Warren," he said. "Okay."

Epilogue

"All right, ladies! Butts in! Bosoms up! Arms out! Fingers together! Show me what you've got! Let's see that showgirl walk! Fast, fast, slow, slow, fast! One-two-three-four!"

"Rita, I wish you'd quit—showing off," Lou Kurian said, panting heavily in the front row. "Can't you wear the 'swoosh' like the rest of us? Anybody that can do this in three-inch heels ought to be *shot!*"

"Quiet in the ranks!" Rita said, laughing.

"I'm only putting up with this—because it turns—Bob on," Lou insisted, still panting.

Smiling, Rita turned around with her back to the

class, so they could see the moves better. "Again! Fast, fast, slow, slow, fast! One-two-three-four! Keep those hips loose—glide—dip—sway those hips!"

"Does it have to be hips, Rita, or can we sway whatever will move?" someone asked, and everybody laughed, including Rita.

I love this, she thought. *I absolutely love this.*

Rita had finally found a space she could afford to rent, and her classes were full all the time.

She realized suddenly that everyone else had stopped dancing, and she looked around.

An officer stood just inside the doorway.

Rita stared at him. "Oh," she said. "Oh!"

She didn't even remember crossing the room, only the leap she made into his arms.

"McGraw, you're here!" she whispered between kisses. "Why didn't you *tell* me?"

"I didn't know. A space came open on a plane out and—"

She didn't let him finish. She kissed him—hard. She didn't care about the details. He was here—after six long months overseas—and that was all that mattered.

"Nothing's wrong? You're okay?" she asked urgently. He'd *said* he was, in every e-mail, every letter, and Bugs had constantly assured her that everybody he knew who was over there with McGraw had verified it. But it was McGraw's first assignment after being returned to active duty. After months and months of standing by him during his rehabilitation, she had ended up keeping the home fires burning after all. And what a wrong way of saying something *that* was. It sounded all nice and cozy. What it was, was hell. It would have been hell even without his mother's relentless disapproval.

"I'm fine," McGraw said. "You're okay? Olivia's okay?"

He leaned back to look at her for a moment. All she could do was nod, like one of those dogs people put in the back windows of their cars.

"I can't believe you're here!" she said, hugging him hard again.

She suddenly remembered the class, and she abruptly let go of him and turned around.

Every single one of the women was wearing the same expression.

"Okay, ladies. I'd like you to meet my husband, Lieutenant Boyd McGraw."

"Aww-www..." they said in perfect unison, and McGraw laughed.

"I just *love* happy endings," Lou Kurian said.

"Rita, can I lock up for you?" Corey asked. "If you want to leave now, that is."

Of *course* she wanted to leave.

"Thanks. Thanks—" Rita said, staring at McGraw again. Her knees were weak just looking at him.

"Did you get what I sent you?" he asked.

"Yesterday. I got it yesterday."

"Did you hold it up to the light and look in the bottom?"

She smiled broadly. "The Mona Lisa," she said.

"I couldn't find one with a cameo. I tried but—"

She abruptly flung herself at him again and held on tight.

"You're not going to cry, are you?" he whispered.

"I think so," she said.

"The keys would be very helpful," Corey suggested loudly, and everyone laughed again.

"Oh, sorry. The keys—" Rita tried to think where they'd be if she had any.

"In your purse," Corey said.

"Oh, yeah—"

She made a dash to get her purse, and she handed Corey the keys to the building.

"Good night, ladies," McGraw said with an impish grin as he took Rita by the hand.

"Good night, Lieutenant…" they all chorused. He couldn't keep from laughing.

He looked at Rita, smiling into her eyes. She saw nothing but love there.

"Mrs. McGraw," he said. "Let's go home."

He drove, which was just as well, because Rita couldn't keep her eyes off him. He was so… everything. Handsome and strong now, in spite of his injuries. And he was all hers. She still couldn't believe he was really here.

He kept giving her mischievous little glances as they rode up Bragg Boulevard.

''What?'' she said finally.

''You'll see,'' he assured her. He didn't make the left turn off the boulevard when he should have.

''Where are we going?''

''You'll see,'' he said again, clearly enjoying himself.

''McGraw, where are we going?'' she asked when he took Route 87 out of Fayetteville. This time he merely winked and reached out to take her hand.

She didn't ask any more questions. There wasn't a place on this earth she wouldn't go with him— happily—in her silver dancing shoes and her leotard or not, and he knew it. They rode into the warm summer evening with windows down, music blaring from the radio.

She began to get some idea of their destination when he turned onto Highway 27—Tino and Earlene's barbecue restaurant. But he began to slow down as he neared the narrow dirt road that led to the ruins of Sadie's house, making the turn with the assurance of a man who perhaps had been here more than just that one time when she had brought him.

She gave him an inquisitive look, but she didn't say anything. His warm fingers tightened around hers. She wasn't looking ahead; she had no wish to see the burned-out house. She was looking at him instead, because he'd become so quiet. He parked under the tall trees and left the headlights on. Rita could hear a lone whippoorwill and a chorus of crickets and cicadas; she could see fireflies hovering near the ground beneath the trees and could smell newly cut hay.

"So, what do you think?" he asked, nodding in the direction of the house, and only then did she turn to look.

Rita took a sharp intake of breath, then opened the car door and got out, leaving him there.

She stood there, astounded. Sadie's house had been rebuilt. It looked the way it used to. Everything was just the same, even the granite step that led up to the porch.

She didn't know what to say, couldn't have said it if she had. She wiped furtively at her eyes with her fingers, and when McGraw joined her, she walked away from him, standing alone and struggling for control.

"You okay?" he asked after a moment.

She nodded, not trusting herself to speak.

"Tino and Earlene had a picture of the place. I think the contractor got it right. My father took care of the legal stuff for me, and he and Tino kept up with the building while I was gone. It took a while to get all the kinks out, but once they got started, it went pretty fast. It's yours. The deed's in your name—''

"Why?" she interrupted, looking at him. "Why did you do this?"

"Because I love you. Because I wanted you to know you always have a place to come home to. The place where you were happy. And I thought maybe you could make some good memories for Olivia here. The kind you have.''

"I—it's...too much.''

"No, it isn't,'' he said.

"You don't understand—''

"Then tell me.''

He came to her, resting his hands on her shoulders. She looked up at him. How could she explain? He had given her the one thing she had believed lost forever. No one had ever done anything like this for her. No one. She didn't deserve it, and she was afraid of such incredible happiness.

So afraid.

"McGraw—''

"Come inside,'' he said. "Come see the rest of it.''

He took her by the hand when she hesitated and led her into the house, switching on a small lamp that sat on a wooden bar stool by the door. The house was empty and smelled of sawdust and new wood. The floor plan was exactly the same—two bedrooms, a living room, a kitchen and a bath.

He didn't come with her. He let her wander around alone. She marveled that there was a stove in the kitchen and a well-stocked refrigerator.

Earlene and Tino, she thought as she closed the refrigerator door, smiling in spite of how close she was to tears.

She looked back at McGraw. Her husband. The love of her life. He stood waiting, and he looked so…worried, she suddenly realized, as if he thought his surprise, while well-meaning, had only caused her pain.

She went to him then, leaning against him for a moment, then reached up and took his face in both her hands. She kissed him gently on the mouth.

"McGraw, thank you…thank you…" And she didn't mean just for this wonderful gift. She meant for believing in her, for trusting her enough to commit himself to their life together. For understanding an aching need in her she would never have dared name. He had given her himself and he had given her *home*. She loved him so much!

"Don't cry," he said, wiping her tears away with his thumbs. "I don't have a contingency plan for crying."

"Sure you do," she said, her voice tremulous. She pressed her face against his, loving the feel of his body, his warmth, his smell. He needed a shave; his cheek was rough against hers. She didn't care. She kissed him again and again, with great purpose and in exactly the way he liked, until he gave a soft moan.

"Take me to bed, McGraw," she whispered. "Now…"

"We don't have a bed," he said, laughing softly.

"You'll think of something, soldier. I just know it."

And he did.

* * * * *

Silhouette ® SPECIAL EDITION®

presents **THE BRIDAL CIRCLE,** a brand-new miniseries honoring friendship, family and love...

THE BRIDAL CIRCLE

by
Andrea Edwards

They dreamed of marrying and leaving their small town behind—but soon discovered there's no place like home for true love!

IF I ONLY HAD A...HUSBAND (May '99)
Penny Donnelly had tried desperately to forget charming millionaire Brad Corrigan. But her heart had a memory—and a will—of its own. And Penny's heart was set on Brad becoming her husband....

SECRET AGENT GROOM (August '99)
When shy-but-sexy Heather Mahoney bumbles onto secret agent Alex Waterstone's undercover mission, the only way to protect the innocent beauty is to claim her as his lady love. Will Heather carry out her own secret agenda and claim Alex as her groom?

PREGNANT & PRACTICALLY MARRIED
(November '99)
Pregnant Karin Spencer had suddenly lost her memory and *gained* a pretend fiancé. Though their match was make-believe, Jed McCarron was her dream man. Could this bronco-bustin' cowboy give up his rodeo days for family ways?

Available at your favorite retail outlet.

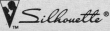

Looking For More Romance?

Visit Romance.net

Look us up on-line at: http://www.romance.net

Check in daily for these and other exciting features:

Hot off the press

View all current titles, and purchase them on-line.

What do the stars have in store for you?

Horoscope

Hot deals

Exclusive offers available only at Romance.net

Plus, don't miss our interactive quizzes, contests and bonus gifts.

PWEB

Silhouette®SPECIAL EDITION®

That SPECIAL Woman!

She's a wife, mother—she's you! And beside each Special Edition woman stands a wonderfully special man! Don't miss these upcoming titles only from Silhouette Special Edition!

❤❤❤

May 1999 HER VERY OWN FAMILY
by Gina Wilkins (SE #1243)
Family Found: Sons & Daughters

All her life, Brynn Larkin had yearned for a home—and a wonderful husband. So when sexy surgeon Joe D'Allesandro offered Brynn a helping hand—and made her an honorary member of his loving clan—had she finally found her very own family?

❤❤❤

July 1999 HUNTER'S WOMAN
by Lindsay McKenna (SE #1255)
Morgan's Mercenaries: The Hunters

Catt Alborak was ready for battle when she was thrown back together with Ty Hunter, the mesmerizing mercenary from her past. As much as the headstrong lady doc tried to resist her fierce protector, their fiery passion knew no bounds!

❤❤❤

September 1999 THEIR OTHER MOTHER
by Janis Reams Hudson (SE #1267)
Wilders of Wyatt County

Sparks flew when widowed rancher Ace Wilder reluctantly let Belinda Randall care for his three sons. Would the smitten duo surrender to their undeniable attraction—and embark on a blissful future together?

Look for That Special Woman! every other month from some of your favorite authors!
Available at your favorite retail outlet.

Silhouette®

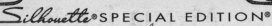
Silhouette® SPECIAL EDITION®

That's My Baby!

Don't miss these heartwarming love stories coming to Silhouette Special Edition!

June '99 BABY LOVE by Victoria Pade (#1249)
A Ranching Family Ry McDermot was capable of caring for his ranch, but was at a loss when it came to his orphaned nephew. Until nurse Tallie Shanahan stepped in to give him lessons on baby love....

Aug. '99 I NOW PRONOUNCE YOU MOM & DAD by Diana Whitney (#1261)
For the Children Lydia Farnsworth would have been happy never to see former flame Powell Greer again. So why was she marrying him? For their godchildren, of course! And maybe for herself…?

Oct. '99 SURPRISE DELIVERY by Susan Mallery (#1273)
Heather Fitzpatrick became irresistibly drawn to the pilot who unexpectedly delivered her precious baby. Now if only she could get her heart—and her gorgeous hero—out of the clouds…!

THAT'S MY BABY!
Sometimes bringing up baby can bring surprises... and showers of love.

Available at your favorite retail outlet.

Silhouette®

Silhouette ® SPECIAL EDITION ®

Myrna Temte

continues her riveting series.

HEARTS OF WYOMING:

Rugged and wild, the McBride family has love to share...and Wyoming weddings are on their minds!

April 1999   WRANGLER SE#1238
Horse wrangler Lori Jones knows she'd better steer clear of Sunshine Gap's appealing deputy sheriff, Zack McBride, who is oh-so-close to discovering her shocking secret. But then the sexy lawman moves in on Lori's heart!

July 1999   THE GAL WHO TOOK THE WEST SE#1257
Cal McBride relishes locking horns with Miss Emma Barnes when she storms into town. Before long, the sassy spitfire turns his perfectly predictable life upside down. Can Sunshine Gap's sweet-talkin' mayor charm the gal least likely to say "I do"?

And in late 1999 look for WYOMING WILDCAT:

Single mom Grace McBride has been spending all her nights alone, but all that's about to change....

Available at your favorite retail outlet.

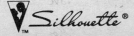
™ *Silhouette* ®

Look us up on-line at: http://www.romance.net   SSEHOW

Coming in June 1999 from
Silhouette Books...

Those matchmaking folks at Gulliver's Travels are at it again—and look who they're working their magic on this time, in

HOLIDAY
Honeymoons

Two Tickets to Paradise

For the first time anywhere, enjoy these two new complete stories in one sizzling volume!

HIS FIRST FATHER'S DAY   Merline Lovelace
A little girl's search for her father leads her to
Tony Peretti's front door...and leads *Tony* into the
arms of his long-lost love—the child's mother!

MARRIED ON THE FOURTH   Carole Buck
Can summer love turn into the real thing? When
it comes to Maddy Malone and Evan Blake's
Independence Day romance, the answer is a
definite "yes!"

Don't miss this brand-new release—
HOLIDAY HONEYMOONS: Two Tickets to Paradise—
coming June 1999, only from Silhouette Books.

Available at your favorite retail outlet.

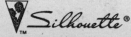

Coming in May 1999

BABY *Fever*

by
New York Times Bestselling Author

KASEY MICHAELS

When three sisters hear their biological
clocks ticking, they know it's
time for action.

But who will they get to father their babies?

**Find out how the road to motherhood
leads to love in this brand-new collection.**

Available at your favorite retail outlet.

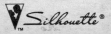